Mari Arden

FLAME

Book One of Fireborn

To my parents - who, by living
their dreams, showed me how to live mine.

To YOU for picking up this book
and beginning this journey with me.

PROLOGUE

I don't have long to live.

I'd never thought about the way I would die before, but if I had, it wouldn't be like this. Alone. In the darkness. Drained.

They told me that I didn't come from this earth. They were only half right. My people were born somewhere else far away. When we arrived we remembered who we were. We remembered the glow and the fire. We remembered the blood. Our purity was gone, but our fight for survival was not.

We were marked. Our blood was black as ash, but they didn't truly understand what we were, and the things we were capable of.

It was the law in every race on every planet only the strong survived. He was weak, the one who saved us all. He was feverish in the head, and his eyes were bright with something that no one could understand. He heard the voices from underground, and he followed them like petals to the wind.

6 · Mari Arden

The nameless one with chaos in his mind had outwitted the gods.

He had a secret, made of fire, bones, and flesh. He helped me to leave clues in the wind, and swept them across the world.

He was waiting for the day when the undying one would die.

* * *

"You got the money?" The voice is rough, and unnatural.

He smiles dazedly at him.

Cold eyes glare back.

A thought crosses his mind that he should be scared, and he feels a slight tremor run through his body. The only thing keeping him upright is the rush of adrenaline from the E-bomb he'd snorted earlier.

He hands the cloaked figure the rolls of Benjamins from his jacket pocket. Fifteen thousand dollars. That's how much his sister gave. There are some hundreds missing he used to pay off his dealer, but it was worth it. He couldn't stand here with the delivery tonight if he'd gotten jumped now could he? Large hands count the hundred dollar bills. He sees the exact moment the man realizes some money is missing. He gulps.

"Hey, man, chill, I can get you the rest later." He attempts to sound cool, but his voice sounds weak and pleading. In the silence, one thought whispers in his mind: he should've snorted more. His heart's pounding now, but it isn't from the drug. It's from fear.

He peers into the voluminous hood, but the deep shadows make it impossible to see inside. Silence emanates from the cloaked figure like a threat. He's reminded yet again of how secluded they are from the city. The nearest road is over a mile away, and the cabin behind them looks old and dilapidated. The trees are bare and the ground barren. The winter breath has wiped it all away. Everything about where they are is desolate and wrong. Even the euphoria from the drug can't hide the tense atmosphere.

When the hooded figure speaks, his voice rumbles with tightly controlled anger. "The deal was fifteen thousand and not a penny less."

He takes a step back. "I don't know what type of deal my sister and her crazy husband made with you, but-"

"The *deal*," the man repeats again with lethal precision, "was fifteen thousand *and not a penny less.*"

"Hey man," he takes another step back. "You can trust me. I can get you that money back. If you would just wait a few days-"

"Wait?" The dark figure's voice continues in a low tenor, but weighs more deadly than yelling. The smirk is felt even though he can't see it. "You don't know who you're dealing with, do you?" The cloaked figure stares hard at him. "In fact, I don't think you know *what* you're dealing with." A chuckle escapes dried, cracked lips.

The sound sends cold shivers down his spine. *Something is very wrong here,* he realizes with growing unease. Every instinct tells him to flee, but he can't move. His feet are cemented to the ground, immobile and heavy.

Suddenly, a strong hand shoots out, grabbing his neck with force.

"Your sister kept you in the dark about a lot of things, it seems." He's rasping for breath, but the hand is ruthless.

"Where is the package?" the figure asks so softly he almost doesn't hear it.

"B-b-b-ack th-e-re," he pants, his hands clawing at the force holding his life. "In the car." His attacker squeezes for a second more, taking a perverted delight in his suffering. When he's released, he falls to his knees, gasping for air. The hooded figure watches him with detached interest.

"Bring it to me," the stranger commands. Then he adds, "If you try to run, I will find you. And you will be very, very, sorry."

He knows it isn't an empty threat.

He stumbles away, terrified. What kind of crap had his sister gotten herself into? But that thought is brushed aside with the nauseating smell of fear. This is the only thing his sister had ever asked him to do, so he's doing it. But after this, he's going to drive far, far away and never look back.

He pulls the car door open, and stares at the small box containing his sister's most precious possession.

Her daughter.

His niece.

The "package" that needed to be delivered. He uses both hands to carry her. She's awake, and staring at him with wide eyes. He met her for the first time a week ago, and in that time he'd grown close to her. Well, as close as a person like him could, anyway. A wave of sadness washes over him as she coos to him. He shakes it off and continues forward to the scariest man he's ever seen. If he hadn't promised his sister, he would've ran with the baby right then, but he doesn't. She'd looked desperate when she made him promise. And he loved her, so he agreed.

He hears crickets and owls in the darkness, but the baby is oddly silent. Maybe she's starting to sense fear. He sure as hell recognizes it. When he's in front of the man, he can't bring himself to let go of the box. Even through the drug-induced adrenaline pumping through his veins, he's having doubts about what's happening.

"Give her to me," the cloaked figure says, staring at the box he holds.

"What are you going to do with her?" he asks.

"What your sister asked me to do, of course." The man moves to take the baby, but his own fingers tighten around the box.

"Where's my sister?" he suddenly asks, afraid. Doubt plagues his mind like darts. Maybe if his sister saw this man she wouldn't allow him to take her baby. He looks dangerous. Before he can say more, the dark figure reaches over to pry his fingers loose. The baby is out of his arms before he can even blink. The large man reaches in with one hand, and lifts the girl into his arms. The empty box is thrown carelessly to the ground. In the darkness there is silence as the cloaked figure stares at her. She is completely still.

Warning alarms ring in his head.

"Where's my sister?" he asks again. A growl of anger erupts, and the man's arm shoots out once more, clasping his neck. This time the pressure is so intense he sees flashes of light in front of his eyes. The man had been holding back before, but he isn't holding back now.

"Dead. And you'll be meeting her in hell." His attacker is literally squeezing the life out of him. His feet dangle in the air, as breathing becomes impossible.

The last thing he sees before his eyes close forever is a bright light, filled with orange flames. When it goes black, he hears the sounds of fire and smells burning flesh.

He was no more.

CHAPTER 1

EIGHTEEN YEARS LATER

I watch as they fly above us. People from all over lined up for days to catch a glimpse. I don't blame them. The TV screen can't quite capture the intoxicating allure oozing out of them like a ripe fruit. Their feet hardly touch the ground before reporters surround them like famished vultures.

The drive thru theater screen looks tiny in comparison to the circular aircraft Ambassador Damien and the other Saguinox arrive in. The ship is round and deceptively flat. It gleams metallic and silver, drawing my eyes to its flashy exterior. No matter how hard I try I can't see any lines where doors or windows might be. Light bounces off the metallic gloss, and it hurts to look closer.

The ambassador is being greeted as if he's a rock star. His mesmerizing looks have been plastered in TV and magazines for months before this day. He's waving to the crowd and flashing a spellbinding smile. Something pink is flying in the air, and hits his chest before falling to the ground. I gape when I realize what it is: a pink, *very* frilly bra. I'm not surprised, but I do feel a little embarrassed. They're *aliens*. Do they even like that sort of thing?

Shaking my head at the woman's boldness, I note the rows and rows of vehicles stretched from the screen all the way back to the gate signaling the end of the Valley Drive Thru property. There's less than a foot between each car. Other people are on bleachers set up from the night before. There are multiple cameras. Men hold some, and others are on stands. One camera is higher than the rest. It's also closer. The crane operator knows what people are here to see: a glimpse of the Saguinox Angel eyes.

The sounds of a second ship flying above us ushers another roar of excitement. I wince, covering my ears from a particularly high- pitched scream. The girl next to me- if "next" means a three-foot space separating us- claps her hands enthusiastically. Her whistles are left unanswered as the ship continues forward, ignoring the frenzy. The mass excitement is building, rising higher with each second, like an orchestra crescendo. We have no conductor to pace our energy, and emotions surge, spilling, and swelling until my insides- and my ear drums- might burst at any moment.

"Oh my gosh, I can't breathe!" The girl "next" to me shouts above the cheering to her friend. "I'm so excited! I can't believe they're going to be here, in our town, in our *school*. Eeek!" she squeals with girlish pleasure. Her friend replies back with similar shrill sounds. *Candace.*

We have Calculus together, but no one would know it looking at the wide space between us. It's crowded. Unusually so, but not a single person thinks to move closer to me.

The second aircraft lands in a cornfield next to us. The screen's split. One half shows images of the ambassador and a few of his cabinet members. The other zooms in on a spot that is probably a door, but it's hard to tell because there are no lines defining it. Someone's trying to talk over the loud speakers, but it's buzzing in the background. The real action is in front of us.

We have an advantage where we are. They call it Lover's Cove. It's corny, and almost no one says it without rolling their eyes or giggling, but it gets the point across. It's a place for lovers. We're on a hill overlooking the drive thru. Vendors are selling their ware like this is a sporting event. I can't fault them though. Even I, Kenna Parker, am toting bloody, almost rare beef patties slathered with cheese, and a deliciously fattening blend of mayonnaise, spicy sriracha sauce, and a touch of sour cream.

The yellow visor over my head is doing a poor job of blocking the heat. It doesn't help that a small cart is strapped onto the front of me like a rectangular backpack carrying sides of cinnamon sticks, fries, and nachos. The mass of people below surges forward, bellowing for more as the ambassador moves closer. Their combined cries overpower Alex's shouts from behind.

"Lemonade!" he yells. "Chucky burgers!" The black Goth clothes and low hanging metal chains are in stark contrast to my yellow, overly bright uniform. His blonde hair is dyed purple at the tips. Being the nephew of the owner lets you get away with things like not wearing the work uniform. I let him promote the product since I've been unable to move for the last twenty minutes. The crowd behind has grown too large to navigate through.

"I bet the students are in the second one!" Candace yells to her friend. The squeals and dreamy sighs following her prediction are enough confirmation. The split screen is now unified. The main cameras face the second aircraft, and two figures appear. The first is a girl. She observes the crowd with confidence. Her blonde brown hair and heart shaped face is as perfect as any can be. She's dressed in a stylish suit. Glowing eyes crinkle as she smiles, waving like a pageant queen. The second figure behind her garners an even louder response.

At first his face is hidden in the shadows, but his eyes glow before his features become visible. He's tall, towering over the girl like a giant. His black hair is darker than the coals we use in the restaurant to smoke meat. When he ducks through the door, his entire face is seen, and a wave of sighs and giggles greet him.

My eyebrows shoot up as I take a step back. He is without a doubt the most handsome man I have ever seen. I'm not surprised because the Saguinox are known for their beauty, but something foreign flutters through my body. It makes my skin tingle. This is such a strange feeling that I tense. Unable to take my eyes away, I keep looking. A square chin and sharp cheekbones make his appearance hard and intimidating. Even through the screen an air of arrogance emanates from his presence. The first word that comes to my head is *intense*. Hypnotizing. If I weren't carrying twenty pounds of food, I would've put a hand over my head and swooned the way that Candace dramatically did. Fortunately the smell of grease has a way of sinking through your skin and into your brain. Right now my brain is telling me that *I'd* be the fried one if I dare drop anything.

"Oomph." Someone bumps into me. Bright blue eyes look down into my hazel ones. "Sorry." He seems surprised. "I didn't see you there." I mumble something incoherent back. Ugh. I'd only been standing here in an extremely yellow uniform for the last half hour. I might've felt hurt if I wasn't so used to it.

He does a double take as he notices the uniform. "Are those *wings* coming out of your arms?" he asks. Instantly, he bites his lips as if he's said something embarrassing. Most people don't come out and say it the way he does as part of the whole Minnesota nice thing, but curiously stare at the odd choice of work uniform. A yellow shirt and flared golden skirt paired with knee high orange and black striped socks and black flats; all of which are mandatory during work hours. The owner Chuck thought it'd be "eye catching" to add small arm accessories in the shape of fluffy, yellow wings that, when paired with the rest of the getup, made you look suspiciously like a giant chick.

He's waiting politely for an answer, and I nod. "Well that's... interesting," he replies courteously. He turns, and disappears into the group. Within seconds, I'm by myself in my invisible bubble, in a crowd of hundreds. I glance back at the screen. Ambassador Damien is waiting to address the crowd. Even though the mayor is speaking, the cameras focus on the Ambassador's side profile. They capture his prominent nose and the golden luminosity sparkling beneath his thick lashes. *Angel eyes,* the crowd chants. It's a rhythm that reverberates in my head. *Angel eyes, Angel eyes, Angel eyes...*

Energy and adoration pour out of every person here with ferocity. Yet, the only thing I feel as I watch his Saguinox smile light up the screen is a sense of resignation.

A lone surfer, barely floating above an empty ocean.

That's what it feels like inside my soul.

CHAPTER 2

At first, the sun blinds me. It's unbearably bright, the sort of brightness that pierces your vision even when your eyes are closed. I shield them, and the wind whips my face, blowing my brown hair behind me. I hear her laughter and I turn. She's waiting, gesturing at me. She's wearing a floral dress, and shielding her eyes, too. Her face is blurry, but I know she's smiling; I can sense it from where I'm standing.

"Over here, Kenna," she yells from afar.

I'm ecstatic. "Mom!" *My voice sounds small in the wind.* "Mom!" *I run to her, but I'm slow. No matter how fast I move she stays in the distance with her dress flowing around her. Wait, I try to say.* I'm coming. *Something changes, and she looks up. Out of nowhere a shadow suddenly appears above us. It's a ship, and its engines are drowning her words. It hovers above her, and she stares at it, transfixed.*

"Mom," I yell again. "Stay there!" Unexpectedly I'm afraid. The ship isn't moving. It's right on top of us like

smog, and I'm not sure what it's trying to smother. A door opens, and stretches to the ground like a ladder.

A figure appears.

At first he's blurry too, but then he takes a step forward and I recognize the handsome Saguinox alien from the drive in. He's not looking at my mom. He's gazing at me. I stare back. Somehow despite the distance, I see his face clearly. His glorious black hair, glowing eyes, and strong chin make me breathless. I can't read his expression, but I don't care. I just want to look at him.

"Kenna!" My mother's voice breaks my spell. She runs toward me, and for one second her face is abruptly in focus. There's fear there. I run forward, trying to reach her. She's shooing me away, but I won't turn back. I won't let her leave me again.

There is a sound above us, like something being unleashed, and I know it's important to run faster. I try to warn her. "Don't look up!" I shout, but she's motionless. She's lost control of her body. Her eyes are wild, trying to tell me something important. The air is chaos around her like a fan is blowing from underneath. Her mouth opens.

It's a trap.

I can't hear the words, but they're in my head.

"What?" I stop in mid motion.

Her face contorts, and the voice is no longer hers. "Run!" it tells me. "Run, Kenna!" I don't hesitate, and I bolt, reversing away from the ship, sensing the danger. Abruptly, I become aware of a thick blackness growing around me. The man from before is no longer by the door, and blackness is leaking from it like a poison. I stumble to the side to avoid it, but it's no use. The dark fog encircles me, floating closer and closer. When it touches me, a cold tingling envelopes my body. I freeze. I don't know if the fog is freezing me, or if I'm too shocked to move. All thoughts disappear when the tingling starts at my ankles and travels to my knees. It moves further up, and I forget everything. My blood is icy, and I'm chilled from the inside out. Dimly, I'm aware of a voice. It's too weak to penetrate through, so I ignore it. There's something stronger calling to me now. The fog is icy cold- deliriously so. How can something so cold feel so good?

"Move, Kenna! Get away!" A feeble sound pierces through my delicious haze. I blink to clear away something nagging my mind. My body sways with the intention to lie down.

"Wake up!" The voice is loud, booming in my mind. The birthmark on my finger burns, and a shaft of heat shoots up my arms, and down my body. The blackness shifts, looming above me, attempting to cave in like a collapsing roof. When I look up I see the dark abyss that waits for me. Its mouth opens to take me...

Wake up!

Cold hands shake me. I welcome the iciness because my body's on fire. Dad's face is unclear at first, but the smell of alcohol drifts into my nose as a pungent breath.

"Kenna, wake up. Whas wrong wi' you?" His voice is slurred, but his eyes are blinking, attempting to focus on me. I sit up, almost begging him to touch me again. I feel so hot. I palm my forehead, but it's impossible to know if

I have a fever when my hands feel even hotter than the rest of my body.

"Hot," I choke out, fanning my face.

He nods. "Feels like a f-f-furnace in h-h-he..." *Here,* he attempts to say, as his words slide together like fluid. "Did y...turn...on..?" His question hangs in midair. I don't need him to say more because a decade of experience has taught me to decipher his drunken code talk.

"I didn't turn on the heat," I reply. It's September in Minnesota, but it isn't nearly cold enough to use the furnace. We can't afford to have heat early. The house isn't big, but I'm lonely at night. *Maybe it's because I'm usually the only one home.* The thought reminds me of a time when it was different, and I push it away as fast as it comes.

Dad rubs his eyes, making them redder. I check the digital alarm next to my bed. It's 4:30 in the morning. He's still dressed in a light jacket.

"Did you just come back?" I ask softly. He nods.

"Did you go with Jack?" I press.

"Don't need to," he answers vaguely.

"You shouldn't be driving when you've been drinking, Dad," I'm unable to hide the exasperation in my voice. It doesn't matter though because I'm talking to air. He's turned away; his mind already wandered off. He circles unsteadily around my bedroom until he comes to a framed photograph. It's the only thing of value I own. He stares like he expects it to move. In the picture, Mom's brown eyes peek mischievously over my head as she hugs me in her arms. The side of her smile is noticeable behind my thick head of hair. He studies the picture. I wonder what he sees. The silence feels immeasurable.

"Dad?" I prod gently in the stillness. He doesn't respond. I walk behind him, my feet soft on the cold floor. I stand quiet as a statue. When the silence becomes heavy with more than just alcohol, I whisper, "Go to bed, Dad."

For a few moments I think he doesn't hear me, but he turns, moving as quietly as when he first slipped in. He walks through the door. He never looks back. My eyes flicker back to the picture that means the world to me. He'd turned it face down.

CHAPTER 3

The reporters and cameramen are visible within a mile of the school. National and local news vans line the streets like spectators waiting for a parade. My rusty 1997 Toyota Camry is nothing fantastic to look at. I'm embarrassed driving by as photographers click away.

I press the brakes hard as the car in front of me makes a sudden stop. I'd been within a mile of the school for the at least ten minutes. Turtles moved faster than we are. I understand that we're the first school on earth to have alien students, but really, is all this necessary? Another bright light flashes between my eyes as a picture is taken. I guess that answers my question, I think.

By the time I arrive at school, my face is flushed with irritation. The parking lot was full, and I had to drive and park on the street. I ended up trying to power walk three blocks with three textbooks on my back. Over forty-five minutes late, I concede that it's not the greatest start to my morning.

I notice a line at the front entrance. Men dressed in blue security suits are checking backpacks and bags. I even see one of those hand held metal detectors they use at sport games. *Is this going to happen everyday?* I wonder. A couple dozen students are waiting to get inside, but they don't seem to mind much. They're probably just happy to miss part of first hour. I'm barely inside the doors when a voice drifts to me.

"I wonder if they're here yet," someone says from behind.

"Probably not. Did you see all the reporters out there? They're still here because they haven't gotten their story yet," a louder voice answers.

"God, did you see the guy, Steph? Hubba, hubba."

"Delish," the second voice agrees. "His name's Rhys, I heard."

"*Rhys.*" She says it with a sigh. "I don't know how I'm going to focus if he's in a class of mine. I'd-" Her voice cuts off as she bumps into me.

"Oh! Sorry. I didn't see you," she apologizes. Her brown eyes are wide.

Embarrassed, I give a small, fake smile. "It's ok," I assure them in the I-don't-care-everything-is-normal voice that I'd spent years mastering.

They walk around and ahead of me. "I swear I didn't see anyone ahead of us..." her voice trails off as the pair moves further away.

I wonder if I stood glued to this one spot, how many people wouldn't "see" and bump into me? What if I start line dancing with my backpack on top of my head? I think sarcastically. How many people would notice *then*? I'm angry enough to try it, but Dr. Bingham's voice booms over the loudspeaker, trampling any idiotic ideas I considered pursuing.

"Students, please report to first hour immediately. There will be no loitering in the hallways. Attendance will be taken promptly at 8:20 am." The principal's nasally voice repeats the announcement once more before a loud clicking sound is heard from behind. Then another. And another, until a hoard of snapping sounds spill inside through the doors.

Cameras.

They'd arrived.

I don't bother to turn around to catch the action. What's the point? I'd probably be trampled to death before anyone realized I was there. Eager whispers and animated excitement ripples through the crowd of students. Ignoring the heightened energy, I take advantage of everyone looking back to sidle to the front of the line.

"Open your backpack, please," the security man says in a bored voice. In a hurry, I do so. I'm ok, until I notice his eyes traveling over a bright, mint green wrapping. My cheeks heat up at the feminine product in my bag. How was I to know there'd be a man rummaging through my bag today? His fingers find a half eaten Twix bar, and an unopened Cheez- it pack, before he finally looks up.

"You're good," he says.

I lift one backpack strap onto my shoulder, and rush away, zipping the bag as I walk. *Note to self: hide everything embarrassing ASAP!*

The classroom door creaks as I slide it open, and a few sets of eyes drift over. When they see who it is, they turn back to the TV, bored. AP English Literature is in full swing by the time I come. Walking over to Mr. Bernard, I whisper my name, "Kenna Parker."

He lifts a hand to his ear. "Eh?" I point to my name on his clipboard. He writes a checkmark beside *Kenna Parker* and adds a "T" to indicate tardy. For a split second, I debate whether I should point out technically I'm on time, but due to external circumstances such as new alien students, I was forced to be late. I decide it's not worth it, and find a seat. A third of the chairs are empty. It doesn't surprise me that some of the students made an opportunity of this momentous occasion, and skipped school. I might've also, but I had to do a cooking demo in Home Economics, and to put it bluntly: I'm bored at home. There's no one to keep me company but a hung over father, and an overly quiet house. Yes, unfortunately, given a choice, I would choose school every time.

The lights are dim because we're watching Romeo and Juliet. It would've been a nice movie had we been watching the Leonardo DiCaprio version, but we're stuck with a movie from 1968. It was so old some of our parents weren't even born yet when it was released. Mr. Bernard had been a young man when this movie first came out, so he didn't seem to notice or care what we thought. Last week he'd spent a good fifteen minutes setting up the old VHS player to accommodate the ancient tape. I wonder how long it'd taken him today.

"O happy dagger!

This is thy sheath; there rust, and let me die."

Juliet's frantic words are said with such desperation I pause to look at the screen on my way to my seat. The intensity in which Juliet stares at the blade she holds leaves me with a disconcerted feeling. I understand her anguish.

I go straight for my usual seat at the back of the room. Even when I'm in the middle of a group, I have a way of making people forget me. At least, that's what it feels like. I hate it, but I can't make someone see me if they don't want to.

A loud snore covers up the sound my backpack makes as it slips from my shoulder onto the floor. I want to sleep too, but I know Mr. Bernard will be planning a pop quiz on the movie tomorrow. It's what he always does, but half the room is dozing off and appears to have forgotten this pattern. Instead I cushion my cheek with my hand, propping my suddenly tired head up. I felt fine seconds earlier, but something about this movie is sucking my energy dry.

The birthmark on my finger itches, and I scratch it. The reddish brown stain starts from base of my thumb on my palm to the tip of my index finger. It's an unusual looking mark, and it's been itching a lot lately.

"What misadventure is so early up,

That calls our person from our morning's rest..?"

My eyes wander to the window beside me. It's hard to resist looking out. Now that fall is here I like to watch the leaves twirl, settling aimlessly about. It's mundane, thoughtless, yet every second soothes me. Today large vans and foreign looking cars line the streets obstructing my view. I stare, but few leaves are falling. Maybe this is the universe's way of telling me to pay better attention to the movie.

A loud knock interrupts my thoughts. Dr. Bingham strolls in looking nervous, and a little agitated. Someone immediately turns on the lights, and it floods the room, forcing a few heads to look up, dazed.

"Daniel! The movie," Mr. Bernard waves at it. A blonde haired boy in the front row jumps up and grabs a black remote. He presses a button, pausing it.

"This is the button for pausing, Mr. Bernard," Daniel explains patiently, showing him. The person ahead of me snickers softly. Dr. Bingham stands at the front, clapping loudly to get everyone's attention.

"We have a new student joining your class today," he begins with a small smile. He gestures to the people at the door. It's then I notice what appear to be two secret servicemen, the assistant principal, and two other official looking men. As if on cue, the two security men part and our first alien student walks in.

Rhys.

Again, the dreamy sighs I first heard when they landed are reenacted within milliseconds of his arrival. It somehow sounds just as loud as before even though only ten female students are in the room. Dr. Bingham seems a little embarrassed by the sighs. His neck gets red, but he keeps his eyes on us. Having the hots for an alien is still a novel idea for many people on earth. I'm not even sure if it's physically possible to *do* anything about it.

Rhys's eyes seemed to glow less in the light. In front of us, they just look abnormally bright. If you scan past him briefly, you might not even notice it. But it'd be impossible to pass over him quickly. His physical beauty is too seductive to ignore, and even though I'm far away, I blush. Biologically we're supposed to notice differences like disfigurement or deformity, but the human eye notices something else too; it notices perfection. Morning sunlight reveals a face that is perfectly symmetrical. This is something no camera can capture; you have to experience it to understand.

He's dressed in dark jeans and a plain forest green shirt that contrasts the olive tones in his skin. The clothes are simple and clean, but he wears them like they've been made for him.

"This is Rhys, er, Doe," Dr. Bingham continues. "Rhys Doe," he repeats more forcefully. I nod in understanding. Like John Doe. Maybe aliens don't have last names. I'm suddenly curious if I'm right.

"He will be here for the rest of the semester with us. Please do your best to follow the guidelines we sent home earlier this month," Dr. Bingham reminds us. The "guidelines" he's referring to was a letter of information detailing what we could discuss with our new "planetary exchange students." The list included human culture, language, foods, music, fashion, and media. It asked students to defer from asking "deep, personal questions" that could threaten national or Saguinox security.

"Welcome," Mr. Bernard greets in a forcefully cheerful voice. It's obvious he has no idea how to handle the new events unfolding in the world, like having an alien student, but he's willing to make the most of it. Maybe that's why the national government chose Minnesota. Minnesota nice extended to extraterrestrial creatures, too.

"Well, um, take a seat." He gestures to the rows of empty chairs. His white hair looks whiter next to Rhys' ebony colored head. "We were just watching a very famous story called 'Romeo and Juliet'. It's, er, a human story about love." Then he looks at Dr. Bingham as if he's suddenly realized something. "Does he need an inter-?"Again, Mr. Bernard stops, not wanting to embarrass his new student.

Immediately, Rhys replies, "I don't need an interpreter. I am still learning your language, but I have been studying it and your culture for many years. If I need help, I know how to ask," Rhys replies. His voice is smooth, syrupy, and holds a hint of an accent I can't place. *Well, duh,* I abruptly think to myself. *His accents from* outer space!

"Oh, great. Good," Mr. Bernard sounds relieved. "Well, welcome again, and take a seat."

"If you need anything, let us know," Dr. Bingham tells Rhys. "They," he gestures to the security, "will stay and-"

"That won't be necessary," Rhys gives him a polite smile. "I'm sure they have other things to do that will be more... beneficial. I think I can take care of myself." His voice is low, but every person including me, strains to hear his conversation. Maybe he notices because his voice gets softer, and I can't hear anything from the back. An older gentleman from the group at the entrance steps forward to protest, but Rhys raises a commanding hand, and he stops.

That's when I notice the air of authority around Rhys.

I straighten, observing his stance, and the control in his body. He reminds me of an uncoiled snake, low and disguised, but hiding something lethal. Rhys' head is bent, but I notice his eyes scan his surroundings even as he listens to Dr. Bingham. Our principal nods a few times as Rhys talks, then looks up.

"All right then," he says in an irritated voice, stepping back from a conversation I have no doubt Rhys dominated. "Have a good Monday." With those parting words, Dr. Bingham leads the small group of people away. When the door shuts there is an uncomfortable silence as we try to absorb Rhys presence. The room feels too small, the air too tight to hold a force like him. When he moves, we shrink back, not from fear but from awe.

Someone clears her throat. "Mr. Bernard?" Arianna raises her hand shyly. "Rhys can sit by me if he wants," she offers. Mr. Bernard agrees, happy for a course of action.

"Yes, why don't you do that, Rhys?" He looks at Daniel. "Turn it on again. We'll be able to finish today." Daniel presses the button and within a second the Capulets are back on screen. This time everyone is awake. It has everything to do with Rhys. Every person is aware of the smooth gait of his body as he moves closer to Arianna. His movements are a combination of fluid motions that are unnatural to observe. Rhys smiles at Arianna, and any girl who sees it grins back, never mind that it wasn't meant for them. He slides into the seat next to her like it's something he's done before. The excited tension in the air is so thick I can taste it in my throat. Insecure stares from the boys. Secrets glances and giddy body language from the girls. It's all mixing together like a heady aphrodisiac.

Come, Montague; for thou art early up,

To see thy son and heir more early down.

Empty desks surround me, but Rhys is closest, sitting two rows ahead and to the right. I try to focus, but my eyes wander to him, noticing the width of his shoulders, and the way the material of his shirt stretches to accommodate his large frame. His eyelashes are so thick I see the black color from where I sit. I can't stop devouring him with my eyes. When I realize I'm acting like a creepy stalker, my hands literally force my head to turn back to the screen. The prince is finishing the final scene.

A glooming peace this morning with it brings;

The sun, for sorrow, will not show his head:

Go hence, to have more talk of these sad things;

I feel a tingling on the side of my face, as if someone is staring. That's unusual. The seconds tick by, and the feeling remains. Restlessness unfurls in my belly. I turn my head.

Some shall be pardon'd, and some punished:

Glowing eyes meet my mine head on. I gasp.
Rhys is looking at me.
His stare lingers for a second more, then his eyelashes flutter down. The moment is broken, and it passes, as if it'd never happened at all. But I know it was real. I can't contain the sudden pounding in my heart.

For never was a story of more woe

Than this of Juliet and her Romeo.

I'm not invisible.
He's seen me.

CHAPTER 4

When I leave Mr. Bernard's class the hallway is crowded. School staff monitors traffic flow in full force. A teacher is standing every few feet calling out students, giving reminders, and trying as hard as the students not to stare at the reporters, bodyguards and government officials that have suddenly descended on Morrison High School.

Snap, snap, snap.

Everywhere I look people are taking pictures. Some carry small cameras, and others are pulling out their camera phones snapping pictures of things like the chair Rhys had sat on and the pencil he'd left behind. Earlier a bodyguard had come to get him five minutes before the dismissal bell rang. We all pretended we hadn't noticed him leaving, but the second he shut the door I heard a collective sigh like nervous tension being released.

I walk to my locker to exchange a book. Everywhere people are whispering and it sounds like the chirping of birds. I hear Rhys's name, but I also hear another name.

Lenora. She's the other alien at our school. I overhear some pompous jock joke overly loud about what other "parts" of her might "glow".

I roll my eyes in disgust. *Really?*

Opening my locker, I search for my calculus book.

Snap, snap, snap.

Are those sounds going to be the only sounds I hear all day?

Snap, snap, snap.

Apparently so.

"Uhm." A throat is cleared.

Snap, snap, snap.

Seriously, that clicking's going to haunt me in my sleep!

"Please excuse me." The voice has a strange accent to it.

I freeze.

"Please excuse me. Would you mind helping me with my locker?" His voice is formal and polite.

For a second I tell myself Rhys isn't talking to me. How had he even seen me? When no one answers him, I turn around.

Rhys is standing less than a foot away. His broad shoulders fill my vision, but not enough that I don't notice the half circle crowd that's suddenly gathered around us. People are pretending not to stare, but I can feel their curiosity. *Why is he talking to her?*

It takes a few seconds, but I manage an answer. "Sure. What do you need help with?"

He gestures to the combination lock on the locker near mine. "I have the correct numbers. I keep turning it, but nothing's happening."

"It can be kind of a nuisance."

"New sense?" He pronounces it slowly.

"Like annoying."

He smiles. "Yes, it is."

He hands me a crumpled piece of paper, and I take it. Our hands brush against each other. I notice his skin is rough and hard. Leathery. Unable to stop myself, I take a peek. His palms have calluses.

He notices my stare and says, "We had a rough landing coming through your atmosphere." I'd heard about that. Each move they've made since contacting Earth four months earlier has been recorded and analyzed by every media outlet in the world. Even the late night talk shows have joined in- putting their own spin on stories, of course.

What do smart blondes and UFO's have in common? You always hear about them but never see them! Well folks, it looks like we'll be seeing our first smart blonde today...

What do you call an overweight Saguinox? An extra cholesterol!

When Jay Leno got wind of their problems with landing, he'd said: *what do you call a spaceship with a faulty air conditioning unit? Come on, what do you think? A frying saucer!*

It wasn't a faulty air conditioner, but facts don't matter in entertainment.

"I did hear about that. Apparently debris from your deflector got into the engine and caught fire?"

He looks amused. "Our deflector was fine. It's a lot less complicated than that. We miscalculated the heat levels in the mesosphere, and one of our main engines burned."

"Oh."

Snap.

We try to ignore it.

Turning my back to the crowd, I clasp his lock, preparing to show him what to do. "Turn it three times to the right then you stop at twenty three. Turn to the left... and right again, stopping at nine." *Click!* It opens. "You try it."

He walks closer until his chest touches my shoulder. He puts his arms around and over my body as if hiding me from the startled gazes of my peers. This close I can smell his clean, musky scent. It smells like a combination of mint, linen and wood. He fumbles with the lock, turning it the way I demonstrated. I look ahead, my heart beating faster.

"It's not working." He sounds a little embarrassed.

I take a peek at the throng of people behind us. It's grown larger.

Rhys's bodyguard tries to look inconspicuous, but it's hard to hide a six and half foot frame. His body's a tall street light among smaller lampposts. His eyes scan the group surrounding us, but remains where he is.

"Maybe you'll just have to help me everyday," Rhys half jokes.

My breath catches in my throat.

He sees something on my face. Suddenly there's a mischievous glint in his eye. "Don't look so scared. I'm not planning on *probing* you."

Whatever awkwardness is between us breaks. I laugh. Letterman had done his top ten alien pick up lines last week and number one was: *wanna get probed?*

"Someone must've shot you with a phaser set on 'stunning'," I quip back, remembering number ten on the list.

"Are you a carbon based model?" *Number eight.*

Putting my hand over my heart, I say, "Of all the planets in all the solar systems in all the galaxies, you had to walk into mine..."

"How about a close encounter with the pantless kind?"

Holding back a laugh I say, "I know you're an alien because you've just abducted my heart."

His eyes sparkle.

Am I flirting? It's never happened before.

I can't stop smiling. "Do you understand everything you're saying?"

"Not quite everything," he admits, with a little laugh. "But according to the T.V. audience that list was very funny."

Snap.

He moves closer to me until he's all I see, hear or smell.

"We don't have things like that back on Sangine," he continues. "We don't laugh a lot."

It's a strange thing to say. I want to respond, but I can't. I see Rhys's eyes with clarity. At first they appear only golden, but on closer inspection they hold odd shades of green and some grays too. The colors seem to shimmer together, intermixing in some spots, and standing boldly in others. Somehow when it all came together, it creates a single golden cloud in each eye. Right now the clouds are shining, beckoning.

I like the way he looks at me.

I like the way he sees me.

"Do you have your schedule with you? I can help you find your next class." Did that sound desperate?

"I know where it is. Let me walk you to yours."

I'm so stunned I nod before realizing what I've done. He pulls me to his side. His mouth's moving and I'm pretty sure he's asking me a question like where my next class is. I can't form a thought other than he's still talking to me. He still *wants* to talk to me. I haven't disappeared.

Not yet.

I feel a rush of relief.

Snap, snap, snap.

"Where to?" He's waiting patiently as if he's asked three times already. He probably has.

"Second floor. Room 240."

His hands clasp my elbow. As if on cue, the crowd parts. *This must be what a rock star feels like.* The bodyguard moves to Rhys's other side.

I wonder if Rhys knows where he's going. "Should I lead?"

He spares me a glance. "I can lead. I'm used to it."

He pulls ahead.

I follow.

People are watching us. I can hear them whispering. I don't care because Rhys is near me. He's real and he makes me feel real, too.

When we reach room 240, he stops with me at the door. Looking at the floor, I try to think of something cool to say. *See you later alligator?* No. He'd wonder why I called him a reptile. *Kenna out?* No, too Ryan Seacrestish. *Catch you later?* Would he think I'd be trying to trip him?

Beep. I look up in time to see him pull out something small and sleek from his jean pocket. He glances at it, and his lips move wordlessly.

His eyes darken. He's not happy with what he's reading. When he catches my eyes, he explains, "Something's come up at work."

"You have to leave." I try to push my disappointment away.

"No. It's something that can wait." He tries to smile again, but it doesn't reach his eyes.

I don't want him to go. Not yet. "You've only been here a few days and they've already put you to work?" I joke.

"I put it on myself." He takes a step back and the warmth between us slowly starts to freeze.

"What do you mean?"

"Trying to fix some things I've done." Something about what he says hardens his face. When he speaks again, he sounds flatter, more distant. "It's, how do you say it? No big deal." His accent is as formal as his tone. He takes another step back. The warmth I felt minutes ago is disappearing with each inch he puts between us.

My walls come back up.

"Thank you." My voice is stiff like his presence.

He hesitates as if he wants to say something. He doesn't.

With a smile that doesn't fool either of us, he turns and leaves. People rush by to follow, but I'm rooted to the floor.

I wonder if I've just imagined it all.

CHAPTER 5

My footsteps sound loud on the hard wood floor of our hallway. It's a habit for me to make as much noise as possible to announce my arrival. At first it was a coping tactic to make sure someone noticed me, but it stayed on even after I realized my strategy wasn't successful.

"Dad?" I call to the emptiness. "I'm home!" There's no answer, but I don't expect there to be. He's usually out at a bar, or at Jack's playing cards and drinking. I was happy when my dad found another widower friend to hang out with, but it didn't take long to figure out that they didn't help each other in the way I thought they would.

My feet continue to make loud, disruptive noises as I move to the kitchen. I can't describe how I do it, how it's natural to pound my feet on the surface like I'm jumping on a bed. It used to feel good to feel the stomping in my knees. Now I worry my knees are going to give in early from daily impact. But that's the thing about habits; they're too comfortable to break.

I open the refrigerator door to take out raw chicken breast. I'm a decent cook. I have to be or else we would starve. The motions are automatic; washing, cutting, and frying. Sometimes we have fresh vegetables. Mostly, we don't. So I pair our meals with bread, rice, or whatever carb I can find. Searching the kitchen pantry, my hands touch more empty space than food. Finally I find what I'm looking for. Ramen noodles. *Score!* I salt the chicken and wait for the noodles to soften. When it does, I pour the soup over the chicken, adding a touch of hot sriracha sauce to liven it up.

I dash up the stairs to check if Dad is home. He is. His body lays spread eagle on top of a futon. He's still wearing the jacket from this morning. An office desk is shoved to one corner, and a shelf that used to hold Mom's favorite books is tipped over. Several books have fallen out, half opened and torn, but no one cares enough to pick them up. Or maybe we care *too* much because it's hard, even after twelve years, to touch things belonging to her. This room used to be an office, but it's converted to makeshift bedroom for Dad. His own room lies untouched, and closed.

"Dad." I shake his shoulder gently. "Wake up. Dinner." He mumbles something about not wanting to get up, but I know he will. Hunger has a way of making even the most tired move. I take two stairs at a time on the way down, landing with a thud. While I wait for Dad to come, I do little chores such as clean the counters, and sweep the floor.

I hear the groan from behind before I see him. "Rough night?" I ask lightly. Dad grunts. We don't talk much about the big elephant in the room: his drinking. The sour stench clings to him like a cloud, but he can't take it off. It's a sickness.

I set the table for two, attempting to find matching silverware. The only things we do as a "normal" family is have dinner together when possible. He's the only father I know, and I love him. But I can't shake the sadness trembling in my heart, that I had lost more than one parent that night. She suffered from a brain hemorrhage. And, even after all these years, we still suffered from a broken heart.

"How was school, Kenna?" he asks in a tired voice.

He doesn't pay attention to the news. He's forgotten there are aliens at our school now. I want to tell him about what happened. I want to tell him someone noticed me. But I don't. Instead I say, "Fine."

He grunts. "Good." His balding head bends as he eats, and his blue eyes flutter down. I remember when they used to sparkle. His beer belly is more pronounced. He needs new clothes.

"Do you want to go to Wal-Mart?" I ask casually.

"For what?"

I shrug. "Clothes." *For you,* I explain silently. He hesitates. "We *can*," I quickly assure him. "I got paid already." He doesn't say anything, but I know he'll go. He works in construction, and soon winter will force them to stop working. Luckily, he inherited this house from grandma and, the mortgage is paid for. He's smart enough to give me half of what he makes to save for the cruel winter months. The other half he spends on spirits to chase his demons away.

"Hey," he suddenly says, looking up. He stands, fingers fumbling into jean pockets that are too tight. "I found this. Here." He puts the object on the table and slides it to me.

I pick it up, holding the ends gently.

It's a locket. I open it. Whatever was inside is long gone now, but I touch the shiny interior, marveling at how warm it still is underneath my fingers. The golden chain holding it is thin and intricately braided. Even in the dim light, it sparkles as I examine the folds. The locket is oval shaped and ruby red. I stare with fascination. Different hints of reds, corals, and oranges jumble together, embedded in stone. Curious, I peer closer. Something tells me to keep looking. For a moment, the colors appeared to have moved. But that's impossible.

I blink.

Wiping my eyes, I check again. Whatever I think I might've seen has disappeared. *My eyes are playing tricks.*

"We found it near you," he says, staring at me. Mom talked enough about how they came across me that night that it doesn't bother me when it's casually mentioned. Without warning, a memory floats into my mind.

Lilac perfume drifts into my nostrils as she holds me in her arms before bed.

"I love you more than anything," she tells me, kissing my head. She traces the birthmark on my finger lovingly. "Finding you was the best thing that ever happened."

"How did you find me, Momma?" She smiles, and it reaches her eyes, filling me with love.

"Your angel dropped you off, and made sure we would find you. You had nothing on but a blanket!" she exclaims, tickling me. I giggle.

"Eeewww!" I squeal. She laughs.

"You were so chubby and round. Your eyes were wide and open. It's as if you were waiting for us," she continues softly. Her eyes grow distant. I reach up, tickling her neck. She smiles and I return it with my own toothy grin.

"Tell me about the ashes!" I demand. That's my favorite part.

"Well," she begins, used to telling me the story. She's a storyteller, and she knows how to make me wait. "Your dad and I had just finished dinner with some friends at a farm. It was a cold winter night, and the roads were so icy your dad slipped when he was trying to open the door for me!" She pauses, looking at me. I giggle at the appropriate moment because that's what she's waiting for.

"He was trying to be robantic."

"Yes, he was trying to be romantic," she corrects. "Well, we were on this road, driving through snow and ice when we see this big flash of light. The stars were so bright in the sky we thought it was a meteor shower. Without warning, Dad swerves off the road and heads straight for it! We drive for a few minutes, following the light. We see a fig-ure-"

"My angel!" I exclaim. She looks down, amused.

"We see a figure that was your angel." She bends close to my face. "... And when he saw us, he disappeared! Whoosh!" Her arms flare out dramatically. "One moment he was there, and the next gone!" She stops, waiting for me to gasp. I don't disappoint. My exclamation is breathy and loud. "There was fire and light and colors and when it was all done, you were on the ground, and the ice had melted all around you." She smiles tenderly, her fingers patting my head.

"You might not have been born in my tummy, Kenna, but you were born in my heart." She squeezes me gently, and I giggle.

"The ashes," I remind her.

"There were ashes on and around you. Some black and some white, like an angel's feathers." She kisses my forehead. "Like fire. And I knew then what your name should be."

"Kenna," I say with a big smile.

"Fire born."

The memory stays long enough for my heart to become heavy. "Oh, ok," I say, answering Dad's expectant stare. "Thanks."

I look away, feeling my eyes blur. The stinging is a familiar feeling. So is the feeling of trapping it in.

"I'm glad I have it," I finish. I want to ask how he found it after eighteen years, but I don't because I don't think he'll tell me anyway. My hands close around the locket. *Now I have two things that I value more than anything else,* I think.

"I'm going to put this upstairs." I don't wait for him to answer. I take the stairs two at a time. Walking into my room, I stop when I'm in front of my favorite picture, the one Dad had pushed down earlier. In it, I'm in Mom's arms, and she's squeezing me tenderly. I remember the exact moment when it was taken. It had been her birthday, but she made it feel like it had been mine.

Gently, I hang the locket around the frame, tucking the ends in a pocket behind the frame. The pendant lies right in the middle of the photograph, encircling both of us the way Mom's arms are enveloping mine in the picture. It feels right to have the locket hold us together like this. A smile touches my lips. Feeling lighter, I return to the kitchen.

"Let's get going before it gets dark," I say as I walk in. Dad's waiting for me and it isn't long before we finish eating. Dinner is a simple occasion for us. Every meal is. The night air is chilly so I grab a hooded sweater, and pull it on. Dad still has his light jacket from the night before, and he patiently waits for me, staring out the door. I don't know what he thinks about when he does things like that. Those moments are secrets that he keeps to himself. I want to help him, but I don't know how to if he isn't ready to help himself.

Within moments we're out the door. The Camry puffs to life after we get in. "I hope it lasts 'til winter," my Dad comments, eying the wheel in my hands.

"I hope so, too," I reply.

It's quiet as I drive. Muted music plays in the background, but it doesn't matter. We listen to the silence. We're good at that.

CHAPTER 6

The second day of the aliens' arrival is as hectic as the first, but this time I'm prepared. I wake up thirty minutes earlier than usual. I remember to hide anything embarrassing in concealed compartments. Noticing the cooler weather, I grab a hat I've owned since the eighth grade. I rush out the door and into the car. When I'm near the school, I bypass the parking lot and go straight to resident parking. Nothing is in my backpack except a few notebooks, and the bounce in my step is made lighter by the smaller weight. See? Prepared.

Out of nowhere I hear screeching tires as a vehicle comes to a sudden and dangerous stop by the curb in front of me. Instinctively, I jump back, hitting the back of my head on the tall white fence. It appears the driver is trying to parallel park, but is having a difficult time. I move further away, knowing it's dangerous to stay close to someone who obviously has no idea what they're doing. After a few steps, I hesitate. I turn back to knock on the window. They're tinted so I can't see inside. One window slowly slides down.

"Do you need some he-" My jaw drops open. I can't believe who's in the car. Lenora turns her lips into a helpless smile, but that's not why my jaw is hanging open wide as a potato sack. She's pushed herself so far back from the pedals that she's almost at a 180- degree angle. I instantly note the right leg is on the accelerator, and the left leg is leaning on the brake. One hand is on the gearshift, and the other is tightly squeezing the wheel. My eyes travel back to hers, and she shoots me a confused look.

"It looked easier in the training video," she confesses.

I smile faintly. "I bet." I'm close enough to see her glowing eyes in detail. They seem to be filled with light, but they aren't hard to look at. Deeper colors of violet and gray swirl in the golden mists like fireflies. They remind me of an aurora borealis.

"Do you want me to help you park?" I ask.

"Would you?" Her smile is sugary, but it doesn't seem artificial. On the contrary, she's making me feel like I've known her a lifetime when I've literally just met her! She puts the car in park. Her little heels click on the sidewalk when she gets out. Dark blue skinny jeans encase long legs, and an adorable buttoned striped shirt is roughly tucked in, giving her a carefree, angelic look. *She's only been on this planet for a couple of days, and she already knows to dress better than I do!* I shake my head, amazed. She hands me her keys, and I slide into the driver's seat-literally. The leather is new and luxurious, and my tights slide right over it. Within minutes I have the car parked.

"Thanks." She takes her keys back. "I'm Lenora. Doe," she adds, almost as an afterthought.

"I'm Kenna Parker. And it's no problem." I smile. "You guys don't have last names where you come from?" I guess.

"No." She giggles. "Am I that obvious? It's just hard to get used to having two names. We practiced it in class, but it still doesn't feel normal," she explains as she walks beside me. Large sunglasses cover her eyes. They're the kind I've seen movie stars wear on front pages of magazines. Based on the number of photographers waiting at our school, she's a star of sorts, too.

She shows me something on her wrist. "*This* is our last name," she declares with a small smile. Before I can get a good look at the mark, she pulls her sleeve over it. I wonder if it's a tattoo. I'm wondering many things as I glance at her expensive clothes and then at the luxurious Lexus I just parked. Where were they getting the money for this? *There's probably some complicated secret agreement between our government and theirs,* I reason. Maybe they traded in their space ships for our cars. Maybe they gave us some secret weapon in exchange for money. Who knows? I doubt I'd ever find out.

Lenora turns her head, searching for someone.

"Where is your brother?" Instantly, I bite my lips to stop them from saying more and wince. Why did I just ask that? Why do I even care?

"Rhys? He's not my brother. We're just here together."
She shrugs. "We were in the same program back on
Sangine, our home planet. We studied human language
and culture. We were the best in our class," she admits
proudly. It's a little odd to hear her say that, but it reminds me yet again of how vast our universe is.

Remembering yesterday, I ask, "Did you guys ever
have a class called 'Late night talk shows'?"

She looks confused. "No. Why?"

I shrug.

"There are so many cultures on Earth. It was hard to
choose which to study first. Our data showed us English
is the fastest rising language on this planet so I decided
to study it. I love all your words!" she gushes. She looks
expectantly at me.

I'm supposed to say something. "Er, thanks. I do, too."

Her smile broadens. "I was so happy when we decided
to contact your government. I even got to say hello to
your president."

I remembered that. CNN had aired a few seconds of it.
That little clip played all over the world. It went viral
within the hour. Lenora's effortless charm gained her instant fame. People were infatuated with Saguinox beauty.
Lenora's face had been on countless print and commer-
cial ads and I doubt she even knew about it.

"People were shocked because that was the first
footage of the Saguinox we had ever seen. It was exciting
and kind of scary." I decide to be honest.

Her gaze is empathetic. "I understand. I hope I didn't
scare too many people then."

"No," I assure her. "Well... kind of."

She scared *me*. Aliens? I'd only seen clips of E.T. and had only heard the Katy Perry song of the same name. Some people thought they were our saviors. Others thought the beginning of the end was near. The controversy still hasn't gone away despite the numerous Senate bills purposed and Ambassador Damien's whirlwind world tour prior to Lenora and Rhys's arrival. I'm still not sure what to think.

Rhys's face appears in my mind. I can't help the smile that tugs at my lips.

"We're happy you're in Minnesota," I tell her.

Lenora beams. "Me, too. I chose this place," she reveals.

I'm surprised. I'd assumed it'd been some sort of long secret negotiation, and they'd chosen Minnesota because we could offer privacy that places like California and New York couldn't.

I'm curious. "Why'd do you choose Minnesota?"

"I want to see snow."

It figures. "The novelty wears off fast."

She shrugs. "They let me choose because it doesn't really matter where we go. It'll still end the same way."

I frown, chewing over her words in my head. "What do you mean?"

She shrugs again, looking away. "It just doesn't matter."

"Do you mean the experience won't be any different?" I ask slowly.

"Something like that."

I wonder how long the Saguinox have known about Earth. When I ask her she answers, "For as long as earth has been around. You're just a baby planet."

"Huh. How many planets do you know about?"

"Many," is her mysterious answer.

"Are those planets inhabited by living things too?" I can't help asking.

She hesitates. "Your government considers that classified information."

"Oh." Right. "Sorry."

"No, it's ok. I'd be curious, too," she admits. "They're still working on an intergalactic agreement between our kind and yours, and then maybe we can talk about things you've missed out on, sitting all alone in your milky day," she beams.

"Do you mean milky *way*?" I ask.

"Yes," she nods. "I'm not sure why you call it that. It looks nothing like milk." She pauses. "Milk *is* that white liquid stuff in the lunch room, right?" she asks worriedly.

I laugh. "Yes. Don't worry. Everything you're drinking and eating in our lunchroom is edible, even though sometimes it might not taste like it."

"Good." She sounds relieved. "We can eat anything humans can. Our bodies are very similar." I want to ask her how that can be, but something tells me that's classified information as well.

My stomach makes an embarrassingly loud grumbling sound. Remembering I didn't eat breakfast yet, I take out a small Ziploc bag from the side of my backpack. Baby carrots were the only snacks in our refrigerator so it's what I pull out.

"Would you like some?" I ask.

"Carrots!" She brightens. "We have something similar where we come from." She takes one. "Why are carrots more orange than an orange?" She stares at it, looking puzzled.

I pause, a carrot half in my mouth. "Um, I'm not sure," I say.

"Ok." Not missing a beat, she continues. "If glue can stick to everything, how come it doesn't stick to the glue bottle?"

I gape at her. "What?"

"Yesterday we were using glue, and it sticks to everything! Why doesn't it stick to the bottle? Is the bottle made of some special plastic?" She sounds serious, and an image of her studying and analyzing a glue bottle like it's going to save the world, pops into my brain. I bite my lip to keep from laughing. As best as I can I answer, I say, "We could Google it."

She looks earnest. "I know what Google is. It's a lot like Nexus."

"What's Nexus?" I ask.

"It's a lot like Google." She laughs.

My giggle joins hers, and for a moment it feels nice to have someone to talk to.

"Lenora," the low voice comes out of nowhere. The hair on the back of my neck stands up, and I know who it is even before I turn.

Rhys.

He's propped casually next to a tree. Dressed in jeans and a light jacket, he wouldn't look out of place in an Express catalogue. It's maddening how attractive he is. He saunters over like he owns the sidewalk. Abruptly self-conscious of the ragged hat over my head, I'm torn between using it to hide my face or throwing it to the dogs wagging their tails next to us.

"How long have you been waiting for me?" Lenora asks.

"A few minutes."

"Sorry. Turns out I'm not so good at parallel parking."

He raises a perfectly black eyebrow. "Really." He doesn't sound surprised.

"Don't you dare say 'I told you so'," she warns gently. "You know I've always wanted to drive a car! It's so much more interesting than pressing a button."

"You're really loving this, aren't you?" He looks amused.

"Yes." She turns to me. "Rhys, this is Kenna Parker. Kenna, this is Rhys Doe." Her words are careful and precise. She's still learning the language, and her accent is thicker than his. I can't help noticing the little smile that's appeared on his face.

In my head I say: *I'm the girl you noticed yesterday. I hope this doesn't sound creepy, but would you mind noticing me everyday?* Out loud I say, "Of all the sidewalks in all the cities in all of Minnesota, you walk into this one..."

"Ready for that probe when you are."

It's official. We're flirting. Even in my wildest dreams I couldn't imagine myself doing this, but I am. I'm giddy inside.

Lenora looks between us, confused. "Is that a new human greeting?"

We exchange a secret smile, each daring the other not to laugh. I bite my lips to keep it in. "No." *Just ours.*

"Oh."

Turning to Rhys before my laughter can burst out, I ask, "How was work yesterday?"

His smile vanishes. "Fine." His voice is curt.

Did I say something wrong? He takes a step back from me. He did this yesterday too, and I'm trapped between calling him out or watching him slip away again.

Another step back.

Another inch away.

Suddenly angry, I lift my chin up. *What's his problem?*

"We should get going Lenora."

"Come on," she says, tugging at my elbow. "We're taking the back route. Reporters are in full swing today."

I try not to notice the way Rhys's shoulder stiffens at her suggestion, and shake my head.

"No, you guys go ahead. I've got to make a stop in the office," I lie. His shoulders seem to relax a little with my refusal. Annoyed, I look away. If I didn't, he'd see the daggers in my eyes.

Lenora hesitates. "Are you sure?"

"Very," I answer truthfully. Rhys doesn't wait for more conversation, and gestures without turning for Lenora to catch up. She looks at him then back to me.

"Hmm," she says.

I don't ask what she means by that and she doesn't tell me.

"See you at school," she says. "We're going to be naughty and sneak in. Shhh." She puts a finger to her lips. "Don't tell the reporters."

"I won't," I promise, but her back is to me. I watch them walk away, wondering how two space aliens could look so beautifully *normal.* I think they belong here more than I do.

Rhys bends his head to her, and whispers. Even from half a block away, I notice they're very close. His lips are next to her ear and if he moved a millimeter more, he'd touch her. An uncomfortable sensation settles in the pit of my stomach.

Turning, I stomp off with my usual clatter, listening to my footsteps and the wind. Out of the corner of my eye, I see Rhys look up.

His gaze is a pool of light; sharp and focused. Behind the surface of his eyes something flashes.

Longing.

I freeze mid stride.

Something hard and fast comes by. It's tires jump over the curb. The truck's so close, I smell the diesel before a gust of wind rushes past, blowing my hat up. It's going to hit me. I open my mouth to scream.

Suddenly a pair of strong arms circle my waist, pulling me hard. I'm pushed away, and I fall to the ground on my back. Rhys is hovering over me, his grip steel tight. Everything happens so fast his nose is touching mine before either of us is aware of our bodies intertwined on the ground.

How did he--?

I can hear Lenora shriek but my focus is on Rhys. For a moment everything stops. I'm tingly all over. His eyes drop to my mouth, and my eyes drop to his. I'm breathing hard, and he hears it because his breath catches in his throat, too. My arms move to circle his neck. *Yes,* I think, and I pull him to me.

We stare into each other's eyes, and I'm hypnotized, as if an invisible bell is calling to me. Pictures flash in my mind. Glowing- everything is glowing. Shining, *beautiful* eyes. Floating in a sea of stars. Warm embraces. And fire. Hot, raging, red fire.

Our lips move closer--

"Are you okay?" I can hear Lenora above me.

We still as whatever transfixed the both of us breaks. He holds me tight for a second more as if it's painful to release me. I don't want him to let go. He does.

My body trembles without his heavy weight pinning me down. Adrenaline pumps through me. Sights and sounds come rushing back. Rhys is up and standing, but his intense face fills my vision. He gives a hand to help me up.

I ask the only thing that comes to mind, "How'd you get here so fast?" It comes out breathless. His eyes drop to my chest where I'm breathing hard. His gaze flickers back to mine.

"I beamed over."

"Really?"

Amusement flickers over his features, making them softer. "No."

"Oh." I wait for an answer. It doesn't come.

"Hey, you okay?" Lenora asks again, touching my shoulder. "That truck almost ran you over!" Her eyes are wide. "Your human body could have died."

"That thought crossed my mind," I reply. It's a lie. The only thing I felt or thought of was standing less than a foot away, staring at me with bright Angel eyes.

"Maybe you should walk with us." Rhys voice is deep.

"I've survived walking for at least seventeen and a half years. I think I'll live another day."

"Still..." Rhys is unsure, gazing back where the truck had been. "What if..."

"What if what?" Puzzled, I peer closer at him.

"What if it wasn't an accident."

My mouth opens in shock as a thought suddenly occurs to me. "You're right. Where's your bodyguard?"

For months there've been reports of Klan members threatening violence if our national government allowed the Saguinox to come. Rumors were they'd already sent death threats to the school and the principal. *That truck could've been aiming for Rhys and Lenora.* Cold dread settles in the pit of my stomach.

"What?" Rhys looks offended. "I don't need a bodyguard. I was talking about y--" Something comes over his face. His lips tighten as if to hold himself back. He takes a deep breath. "Yes, that truck could have been an attempt on our life."

Lenora opens her mouth to say something. He silences her with a steel look. I frown.

"You need to let someone know, Rhys."

"We will," he promises. "As soon as you walk with us."

My first thought is *now* you want me to walk with you? After we've just discussed possible assassination? I don't feel fear though.

I feel confused.

Rhys is sending so many mixed signals, I can't tell what's genuine and what isn't. There's so little known about Saguinox culture. For all I know this could be a routine Saguinox courtship. He walks ahead, turning expectantly.

"He leads and we follow," Lenora tells me.

"He leads," I repeat.

"Always."

A student walks by, and I can hear faint music blaring from her headphones. She's heading to our school and we follow quietly behind. Katy Perry's "Hot and Cold" plays on her ipod over and over again. I can hear it through her headphones.

I stare at Rhys's broad shoulders. I think about yesterday and this morning.

It's the perfect theme song to accompany our walk.

CHAPTER 7

My morning sucked. I'd burnt the cake I'd baked in Home Economics. The teacher scolded me for not paying attention because I was supposed to watch the timer. I'd been thinking about a certain alien instead.

The lunchroom is crowded by the time I arrive. I didn't pack food, so I wait in line with a tray. The plan is to get lunch, then head over to my little dining area a.k.a the corner couch at the hip and happening Morrison High Library. The process usually happens like this: I get my food, sit at a corner of some lonely and deserted table, sneak a few suspicious glances here and there, waiting for the opportune moment to sneak off, which tends to happen almost immediately upon sitting, dump edible parts of lunch in the bag and casually leave as if I had not done what I just did. The plan works every time. There's a plus side to not getting noticed; no one sees you when you go.

I'm relieved to see today that our pizza came in a triangular plastic container. I smile. The universe is rooting for me. Maybe it's trying to make up for giving me such a rotten morning. Grabbing an apple, and some silverware I pay the cashier and leave the line, heading straight for the furthest table.

I'm so intent on my destination that I don't see the body until it's already bumped into me, knocking the slice of pizza backwards.

"Oh, I'm so sorry! I guess I wasn't watching where I was going. I- hi, Kenna!" I look up after assuring that my pizza is okay.

Seeing who it is, I smile. "Hi Lenora."

"I'm glad I bumped into you," she beams. "Girls," Lenora waves to the group of admirers behind her "this is Kenna Parker. Kenna, this is Holly Jenns, Grace Spots, Madison Shine, Arianna Lee, and Bree Rose Whitmore!" She grins excitedly. "Bree has *three* names!"

I'm not sure how to respond to that last bit of fun fact. "Cool." I try to sound enthusiastic. She notices the tray in my hands.

"Would you care to sit with us?' she asks.

I hesitate, and she pounces, sensing the refusal before I can.

"Come on, you have to, Kenna! You were such a life saver helping me park this morning," she pleads.

I don't point out who really saved whom earlier. Unbidden, I remember the feel Rhys's arms around me, hard and encompassing, like wings. I want to brush the invisible sensation away, but they linger like frost.

"It'll only be for twenty minutes." Her eyes are luminous, and in spite of me, I find myself wanting to give in.

Almost in a trance, I nod. *I could give it a try,* I think. Maybe it'd be different with someone not from Earth. The cynic inside me thinks: *not.*

"Where are you planning to sit?" I inquire.

"Oh, our usual," Lenora answers happily.

My eyebrows shoot up.

She's only been here a day and a half and she has a "usual" spot already? I have to give the girl credit. She knows how to work this intricate social hierarchy like nobody's business.

"Over there." She points to a table right in the middle of the lunchroom. It's a prime spot, guaranteed to receive attention. I don't mind though. It doesn't matter where I sit, invisible is still invisible. I should be used to that fact, but I'm not. What teenage girl likes to feel unseen? Hidden? It makes me feel like less of a person. Imaginary.

Except when I'm around Rhys.

Then I feel too much. Soft. Confused. Giddy. Real.

I follow the girls like a pet resigned to her fate with an overanxious owner. Grace and Holly hurry to sit next to Lenora at the table, and if I didn't witness it, I wouldn't have believed it. Oddly, I understand. I usually don't like cheerful, overly excited girls like Lenora, mainly because it's hard for me to relate to them. However, I'm strangely comfortable around her. Her presence feels like warm soup during a cold Minnesota winter, or a cozy bonfire on a cool summer night. It just felt *easy* to be with her. Simple. Effortless.

We huddle around her like moths to a flame. Before she can say another word, Holly blurts, "Mike has a crush on you."

"Half the school does," Madison adds with a wistful sigh.

Lenora's looks confused.

"What is a crush?" she asks.

"It's when someone has the hots for you," Grace answers.

Lenora's brows pinch together in a frown.

"It's a good thing. Trust me," Grace assures her. "It means he likes you."

"Ah." Lenora smiles in understanding. She flushes a little with embarrassment.

"Mike is our star quarterback," Madison explains with wide eyes. "He's probably going to the NFL in a couple years." The girls giggle. Lenora shoots me a look. I shrug. Football is beyond me.

"What is football?" she asks slowly, pronouncing it like a foreign word, which for her it was. Silence. There's a moment of quiet as every girl at the table reflects on what they know about the sport.

"A bunch of guys running around trying to catch a ball," I finally suggest when no one breaks the quiet. Grace and Holly turn to look at me, a little startled by my presence. The brief introduction from minutes earlier seems to have dissipated in their memory. The Forgetting, as I call it in my head, didn't take long to kick in. I figured out the pattern to the weirdness. If I don't talk, then the group feels like I'm not there. The group misses me- literally. There were even moments before where someone's eyes had flickered past and over me as if I had melted into thin air.

"Yes, that about sums it up," Bree agrees, pulling me back to the present, smiling sweetly.

The corners of my mouth turn politely back, but it's hard to look at her without remembering our friendship in kindergarten. I know it's ridiculous to hold a grudge about something that happened when you were five, but Bree really hurt me. She always stayed sweet, but it was never the same. I recalled her reluctance to play, her bouts of ignoring me without meaning to, and forgetting important play dates. The strange thing was it didn't seem as if she *wanted* to forget me. It just sort of happened.

The same cycle happened to every friend I attempted to have. They were all nice, but they all shared something in common: they made me feel forgotten. Abandoned.

"You'll have to show him to me," Lenora announces. That's the opening the girls needed. Madison squeals, revealing she knows *exactly* where he is. Stalker much? She insists they ditch lunch to find him. The rest of the girls readily agree, and within moments a plan is devised to stake out the gorgeous football star destined for NFL glory.

I don't say much because it doesn't matter what I think. It only takes me five minutes to note that Lenora isn't immune to whatever I have. Her eyes go right through me to wave to some friends, and that's all the evidence I need. Standing up, I plan to leave quietly and head to the library, but my loud stomping alerts Lenora.

"Kenna? Hey! Where you going?" she asks.

"I've got some things I have to do at the library," I answer vaguely.

"No, stay," she stresses. "We have a plan! We're going to..." Her voice becomes mute in my head as she explains what they're going to do. I'd been there the whole time and heard every word of it, but I let her continue.

"No, that's ok," I say when she's done. "Important things at the library can't get done by themselves." I don't mention what the "important" things are, and she doesn't ask.

Instead, she gives me a perfect smile. Her eyes widen, and the purple spots in them seem to grow more intense. "Stay."

I stare at her, feeling a rippling sensation that I can't name.

Her pupils become enlarged, drawing me deeper.

My mind is literally swaying toward her, reaching out to take what it can. Strangely, I *do* feel an overwhelming urge to stay...

Clank! A loud crashing sound abruptly reverberates across the entire lunchroom, and I start, breaking my gaze away from Lenora. There's a second of frozen silence as everyone looks at each other, unsure of what just happened.

"Fight!" Someone suddenly shouts, breaking the tension.

Instantly, my eyes search for the cause of the commotion. Students are standing, staring at a spot across the room. Usually, I don't care about something as stupid as a fight, but something propels my body forward. I take a few steps toward a crowd slowly gathering.

"What the heck," Madison's squeaky voice comments from behind me. More students get up to see the commotion. I tip toe, stretching my five foot four inch frame as high as I can. Someone's in front of me though, and the top of my head barely reaches his neck.

"Is that... is that *Rhys*?" Bree suddenly asks, bewildered.

Lenora makes a soft sound, and then she's rapidly walking, brushing past me. Feeling a flare of uneasiness, I squeeze myself between bodies, rushing after her. People hear her coming because they make an aisle for her to pass by, still flashing looks of awe and curiosity. They aren't as courteous to *me* though, and I have to jab and poke my way through a few smelly bodies to catch up with her.

When we're near the cafeteria entrance, Lenora halts. I almost bump into her, but she uses her arm to catch me. There is a tray on the ground in front of me, and food is splattered over the glossy floor, like it'd been thrown down. Some guy is next to the mess, his shirt drenched with liquid. Despite his fake tan, a blush of shame or anger- maybe both- cover his face and neck. His mascara- laden eyes, are blinking rapidly, trying to control tears slowly forming. My eyes search and find Rhys standing less than two feet away. He's between him and another student. Rhys's stance is forceful, yet his hands are deceptively relaxed by his sides.

"This isn't your business, alien freak."

I recognize Carver's hard voice, and I can't help the rush of anger shooting through me as I stare at his hawkish face. He and I have been in the same class almost every year since kindergarten, and with each passing year his bullying worsened. Carver's wide shoulders, efficiently used for football the last four years, betray him, trembling slightly under Rhys's steady gaze. I can't help the smirk of satisfaction curling my lips. My eyes go back to Rhys, marveling at how secure he looks in the face of Carver's anger.

"He isn't your business, either," Rhys replies calmly back, referring to the guy still on the ground. I finally remember his name is Seth.

"That twink is spreading rumors and shit about me so it *is* my business." Carver moves closer to Rhys. "Get out of the way." Rhys looks at him for a moment longer, contemplating. I don't know what he's thinking, but I hold my breath, watching what he's going to do. To my utter disappointment, Rhys steps to the side. Carver rushes past him.

Hands curling, he mutters to Seth, trembling on the floor, "You trying to say I kissed you, you shit face? Kiss *this*." He raises his fist like he's going to hit him. Years of watching Carver bully other people flash before my eyes. Unable to control myself, I break away from Lenora's grasp and shoot forward. I never get to figure out what I might've done because Carver is suddenly pulled back.

Quick as lightning, Rhys twists one of his arms behind him, arching his body forward.

"Only a coward hits someone when they're down," Rhys hisses. Roughly jerking him up, Rhys turns away from us, his broad back hiding Carver's struggling body. Using his foot, he kicks him, and Carver falls like a domino to the ground.

Dr. Bingham's loud footsteps alert me to his presence. He takes note of Carver and Seth on the ground, and Rhys standing less than a foot away from them. His lips thin in anger.

"What happened?"

No one answers. Finally, Carvers speaks. Spitting as he stands, he says, "A misunderstanding." It's clear Dr. Bingham doesn't believe him, and his eyes rest on Rhys with suspicion.

"I think it's sorted out now," Rhys answers in a low voice.

The two security men from yesterday arrive next.

Dr. Bingham looks between them. "I'll take these two down to the nurse. You can take *him*," he instructs, his fingers gesturing lightly toward Rhys. The pair nod, but don't motion Rhys over. It's clear they can't make him do something he doesn't want to do. Maybe they signed an agreement, or were told to handle the new aliens with care, but either way no one makes a move.

Rhys watches someone help Seth up.

Seth doesn't utter a single word, but I see him glance at Rhys's from the corner of his eye as he's standing. His eyes shine with curiosity, but they also shine with something else. Confusion. Gratitude. Admiration.

I wonder if my eyes shine that way right now, too.

Seth limps away.

When my gaze returns to Rhys, I feel a mixture of many things I can't deny. The vivid feelings swirl inside me like a typhoon, threatening to fill me with something I'm too afraid to name.

"Rhys." Lenora's voice is so soft I'm not sure if he hears it.

He walks over, looking at her with an unreadable expression on his face. The group of onlookers move, shifting to accommodate him. When he reaches us his gaze travels to me.

Sucking in a breath, I tense, feeling the vibrations of his gaze. I hear the pounding of my heart, and I want to say his name. *Rhys the one person who can see me.* The thought fills me with a strange yearning. For a moment we're trapped in each other's eyes. I can't think except to wonder what *he's* thinking.

Swallowing, I say, "Saving two people in one day. You're an alien hero. They should make a comic book about you." I'm babbling. I never babble. The feelings inside me are making me anxious.

A smile touches his lips. "What would they call me?"

I answer immediately. "Golden Eyes. You can beam to the rescue of any damsel in distress by blinking your eyes."

He laughs. People are staring. Rhys notices because he gestures to the two security men. They come closer, locking us in.

"I can be your sidekick. Invisible woman. The bad guys won't notice me until I've already captured them. We can have a dog, too." I can't stop the words pouring from my mouth. I hear them in my head. I sound ridiculous. Where's the cool, confident girl from before? The one who'd actually *flirted*?

She's gone.

She's seen something wonderful, and she's gone into hiding. She's also talking in third person. *Jeez, even my mind is babbling.*

"The dog should be a golden retriever. It'll match the theme." Word vomit. I want to kick myself.

Rhys is staring at me. He comes closer so only I can hear him. "I can look at you all day, Kenna."

His whispered confession gives me goosebumps. Did he mean listen? I hope not. I'd take look over listen any day.

He sighs. "I should go."

Lenora nods. I don't trust myself to say another word. The two bodyguards follow him out.

In the silence, their footsteps echo like rain on pavement. My eyes remain on Rhys's back until he disappears through the doors.

I feel an unyielding urge to follow.

CHAPTER 8

I'm standing outside their bedroom door. I can hear them arguing inside. Guilt racks my conscience. My birthday party is expensive, but I want it anyway. I press my little ears to the door.

"... Already a month behind our electricity bill! Do you want them to shut it off again?" His voice is angrier than I've ever heard it. Mom answers, but her voice is soft like always. I wish I could hear it.

Suddenly time flashes forward, and the door is open, but I don't want to go in. It's my birthday, and I know what's inside. I recoil, but an invisible magnet pulls me forward. She's lying on the bed, perfectly still. Her motionless body is cold. I know it is because the room is chilly, and when I breathe I can see my breath like a white flower. I whimper, my lips trembling with fear even though I've already seen this image before.

"Mom," I whisper, but I don't expect an answer. When I'm close enough to peer into her face, I shut my eyes. The image appears in my mind anyway. Her wide hazel eyes *unblinking, her face paler than the white sheets she's on. A solitaire rose plucked too soon; that's what she looked like in her nightgown.*

Lightning flickers with a dizzying intensity, followed by thunder. The sounds echo in the dark room. I'm not afraid of storms, but something tells me this is no ordinary storm. Unease ripples through my body. Thunder booms again, and I feel the earth move. The ground cracks open, and I unclench my eyes in time to see my mother's body falling into the hole. I run to try to catch her, but it's no use and I fall after her. The gap is filled with light, and I'm dropping in a glow so strong that it burns me. Just as fast as it comes, the light is dimmed. I fall hard on my knees, and my skin is sliced open. I clutch my knees, wincing from the pain.

Thick gray walls surround either side of me, and the corridor I'm in stretches for a few feet more before a black door halts it. A small golden circle with diagonal lines running through it is red against the dark door.

A sharp scream pierces through the walls, and I jump back, instantly alert. The screams make the hair on my body stand straight. Goosebumps cover my skin when the third scream reverberating through the walls abruptly stops, like the person screaming has suddenly lost consciousness. I move back, wary, and frightened.

My eyes drift back to the black door in front of me. Curious, I want to open it, but another part of me is shrinking back, begging me to stay put. The decision is made for me when the door suddenly opens, and a robed figure strolls through. His black hood is long and deep, and nothing can be seen but shadows and hidden silhouettes. He pauses, and I know he can see me. Perhaps he even senses my fear.

He folds his hands in front of him, but it's nothing but fog and murky smoke.

"Kenna." The low voice echoes all around me, bouncing off the walls and into my eardrums where it stays in my mind, buzzing.

"Who are you?" I'm surprised that my voice doesn't crack. Even as I ask the question, I know the real question I should've asked was: what are you? Because I know he isn't human. His body drifts off the floor like a weightless cloud, and his voice sounds like thunder. Instead of answering, he floats higher up, until he looms above me like a malevolent spirit, which I'm sure he is. He lifts his hands, and a shudder passes through my body.

The iciness is back. It starts from underneath me, and it spreads around me like the flapping of a wing. Every second brings more cold, and it is engulfing the space around and inside me. I start coughing. With blinding clarity, I suddenly know what he is trying to do.

He is trying to choke me to death.

He doesn't touch me, but the iciness does, swirling around me like a chokehold. It wraps itself tighter around me, and I can't move. I'm literally frozen from the cold and from the invisible arms that are strangling me with an arctic bitterness.

Keep moving.

Instinct takes over, and I start squirming, thrashing my head in a wild dance, and attempting to find oxygen in an airless space. I curl my fist, and the scar on my finger is burning. I'm imagining the warmth of a fire, the heat of a blaze. It's so cold it's difficult to blink. The image of a perfect flame flickers in my mind. It's orange with swirls of red, and underneath the swirls are roots so intensely blue it reminds me of an ocean. I envision the flame in front of me, stretching to the ice, burning it with all the ferocity I feel. My head's pounding with the strain to hold the image, but I do it.

I see the fire building around me, licking away the cold and replacing it with sizzling warmth that gathers at my core. It grows hot. I look up. I picture the flame shooting straight through the demon, and abruptly it appears before me, as perfect as I have imagined it. It turns into a fiery arrow and with a cackle it shoots itself right through the middle of the demon.

He anticipates it, and he slides into the wall like the shadow that he is. The fire arrow continues to the black door and breaks into little pieces when it touches the door. He quickly appears again, closer, and harder. His laughter is loud in my head.

"Is that all you have?" he taunts. He lifts his hands again, and a twirling tornado spins out between his fingers, coming straight for me. I can't move, and when it finally touches me, it feels like it's sucking the life out of me, spinning and spinning, until it takes everything.

Something ancient and old is inside me, vibrating from the threat. It tells me to rise up, to stand as tall as a dragon. Magically the image is there: a hundred fireflies, glowing with orange and red embers. As my eyes strain the image attempts to come to life in front of me, but it's faint near *the dizzying tornado. The cyclone is consuming the fire I'm attempting to make. His laughter continues in my head. The cold is winning again. The invisible smoke filled with arctic wind shakes all around me, cracking the firewall around me. It stabs at me, creating thick airless spaces wherever it touches.*

I squeeze my eyes shut, and with a last burst of energy I imagine myself erupting from the icy hands holding me. I imagine my fireflies swarming around him, consuming him the way he had consumed me. Something is ripping inside my hand.

One moment I'm there, and the next I'm on fire.

Chapter 9

Hot.

It's feeling very hot. A bead of sweat rolls off his skin, and he wonders why he can even notice it when a hologram of Malachi is right in front of him. Most people would be trembling, especially if they knew what he knew. But he's not, and the heat is so damn irritating. He catches the drop of sweat, breaking it with his fingers. Malachi's glaring at him, yet he takes his time looking up. Malachi's thinking he has a death wish. Maybe he does.

"Are you sure this human is the carrier?" Malachi asks again, his rumbling voice, rupturing with his anger.

"Yes," he answers, sounding more bored than he wants to. "Armin says that last time her mind fought with fire. It can only mean that the fire crystal is inside."

"Your sources have already been wrong twice," Malachi snaps, taking a couple steps closer. The image crackles a bit then reassembles. "Two dead bodies and no crystal. What makes this time any different?"

A hundred answers come to mind, but he silently counts to ten to make sure he says the right thing. "They've been able to get their hands on something that is proving to be very... accurate."

A low groan is emitted, and they pause, glancing at Armin. He's been at it for longer than normal. He see sweat building on Armin's forehead. Soon he'll be drenched in it. Armin's sitting on a chair, both hands deceptively still on the arms of the chair. His eyes are wide open. Only bouts of rapid blinking belie what is truly happening.

They're all killers.

Blood stains the fingerprints of every single one of them.

Armin's weapon is his mind. He can kill with it. Armin's *already* killed with it. Sometimes he wonders when the blood will haunt Armin's mind, the way it's haunted his own.

Whimpers from the human girl chained to the wall interrupt his thoughts. Two guards stand by her. She sounds hoarse and weak. Her tears are dried up, and her voice has faded with her screams. The ruby red slave dress hangs on her thin frame, and it almost brightens the ghastly pallor of her pale face. Almost. The crystal's taken too much of her life energy, and when Armin takes her blood she'll be nothing but a corpse.

Malachi is abruptly no longer interested in him. His hologram image turns away, watching Armin. The hologram reveals clearly every detail about Malachi. He's a distinguished looking man, older, but with a full head of dark brown hair. Shades of gray sprinkle his hair, embellishing it like a crown. A hint of a mustache lingers above his lips, creating an aristocratic look demonstrating his royal heritage. He's the King of Sangine. Commander and Chief. Prince of the Crystal. He's invincible. Nothing can destroy him.

With an agonized shout, Armin jerks awake. A large vein is visible near his eye, throbbing with what he's done. Armin's gray eyes find him first, and then to Malachi. A flare of fear flashes in them before he hides it.

"Well?" Malachi prods.

He swallows. "She... got away."

A muscle ticks in Malachi's jaw.

"Sir," Armin says, his usually strong voice soft in the silence, "she pulled herself out at the last second. She's obviously responding very well to the crystal. I was very close--"

"Close isn't close enough," Malachi bites out. "You've been trained your whole life for things like this, dream walker, and it sounds like *she* doesn't even know what she is!" He pauses, his chest heaving with rage. The look in Malachi's eyes chills him to the bone. "How can a mere untrained girl beat a Saguinox warrior?" he asks. "How?" he presses when no one answers.

Malachi lets the question linger in the air. The King comes closer to them, breathing heavily. He's desperate. Malachi tries to hide it, but he can see through the façade. Malachi needs the crystal.

After a lengthy silence, Malachi gains control of his temper. "You all are my most gifted warriors. It saddens me that this day has come." His glowing eyes became scarlet. "Everyone leave."

Before they can leave, he steps forward. His heart twists with heaviness. "Your highness," he begins in an unwavering voice, bowing slightly "we have been trained from birth to be our world's greatest soldiers, and our enemy's greatest fear. We were raised as brothers, Armin and I especially. When he fails it's as if I have failed also." He looks up. "Let me carry half his punishment, and I promise you we will not fail you again."

He can see Malachi contemplating the request, and he knows Malachi is reluctant to allow it. There are *some* benefits to being his favorite.

"That's not necessary," Malachi finally answers. He smirks at Armin before looking at me. "At least I know I can trust *you* to get the job done."

He nods with confidence. "Yes."

"Bring me the carrier."

His face remains expressionless even though his fear is growing.

"Yes," he vows.

Malachi glances back at Armin, noting his pale face and glazed eyes.

"Finish the girl," he nods in the direction of the enchained human who is half unconscious. Armin doesn't wait to be told twice before he pounces on her. She's hooked up to a machine. A guard presses a button. Instantly, a river of blood flows through its plastic tubes.

Another guard waits until its sufficiently filled before un-hooking the end. A spray head is attached to it and Armin opens his mouth, bending like he's going to drink from a human beer bong. Armin's body trembles in antic-ipation. When his mouth finally closes on the opening, he sucks at it like he's drawing in air, absorbing the liq-uid in a frenzy. Scarlet blood dribbles down, staining Armin's neck and shirt, but his need is merciless. Armin's desperation seems endless.

Watching Armin, something steely and hard unwinds inside him: rejection. Disgust. When he turns his eyes away, they land on Malachi who watches Armin with a satisfied smirk. Drinking blood is a privilege that Malachi allows for a select few. Armin makes a desperate sound, and he's not surprised when Armin pushes the Saguinox away. Swaying, Armin reaches for the girl, trembling to fulfill his thirst. Without hesitation, Armin opens his mouth, revealing short canines that are barely visible.

Like the animal he's suddenly become, Armin bites the softest part of her body: her neck. Desperation and the force of his hunger give him a rush of strength. Ripping through skin and tissue, he gorges himself on her flesh. Her terrible screams fill the small room.

Malachi laughs.

He's still; knowing to show any weakness is to jeopar-dize everything he's worked for. He endures her cries in silence. After Armin is done, he slumps to the floor, ex-hausted.

"Help him to his room," he orders. When their foot-steps become nothing but echoes, he checks the girl's pulse. It's hard to find it through torn skin and blood, but he manages. The pulse is weak, but still there. His heart clenches with dread for her.

"Put her with the rest of the slaves," he says softly to the nearest guard.

"Kill her and be done with it," Malachi snaps. "We need healthy slaves, not half dead ones."

Rigid, he nods. "Yes, your highness."

He holds her neck in his hands, feeling arteries and bones. He pretends to look at her, but he's pushing his mind away, going to somewhere no one can reach him: his memories. He's inside one memory in particular. Her voice fills his mind, and it's what he holds onto as he slowly chokes the girl to death. Within seconds the light in her eyes darken, never to shine again. He shuts her eyes as if to make it better, but it doesn't fix anything. He knows her face will echo in his dreams just like all the rest. A guard drags her broken body through the door to a furnace that makes useless things disappear.

Malachi makes a sound to get their attention, baring fangs that glint in the artificial light. "I will be arriving in a month. Make sure the fire crystal is ready."

He bows, desperate to leave.

"Oh, and Rhys?"

He pauses, turning back to face his commander.

"Don't disappoint me," Malachi says with deadly calm.

The invisible threat hangs in the air.

"I won't."

CHAPTER 10

"Fire! Fire!"

My scream vibrates against the walls as I shriek and jump out of bed. I scan the room wildly, looking for something to put out the sudden blaze that's consuming my bed sheets. An oversized coat hangs on my door, and I pull it, thrashing it against the fire that's threatening to take over my little corner of the house. I use the coat as a weapon, beating the flames like a boxer. Luckily, it doesn't catch on fire, but I wonder if it's enough. I scream when the coat is unexpectedly pulled from my hands, and sinks into the center of the blaze. A soft eruption signals its demise, and I panic, screeching.

A flame jumps out at me, blocking my only path to the door. Gray smoke is gathering, attempting to leave, but there's nowhere to go. The fire has spread to an old wooden nightstand, and roars louder as it devours more energy.

I swear, dodging another flame. I pound the thin walls with my fist.

"Help!" I shout. There's no answer, and no movement, but I'm hopeful. Then I remember that it's Friday night, and no one is home but me. I cover my mouth and nose with the bottom of my shirt, and rush to the rectangular windows overlooking the street. They're all side-by-side, forming a makeshift balcony. I pick the one to my right, tugging it to open. We locked them in anticipation for the winter, but I use all my strength to crack it open any-way. The old locks resist me, and I heave, trying again and again.

Finally, I give up, and punch the glass with all my might. I don't know what I expect to happen, but I don't wait for the pain to subside before I attempt it again, on all three windows. My knuckles literally feel like they are ringing underneath my skin, but that isn't enough to stop me from using my shoulders, and then my whole body against the glass. I can hear the fire behind me, and I don't glance back to see how big it has grown because then I might give up. I don't want to give up. If I did, my dad would too. Then our whole family would be gone. Given up to whatever flames life had thrown at us.

With this last thought, a surge of energy quivers through me. I resume my concentration on the third win-dow, grabbing the plastic chair next to me. Lifting it high, I slam it against the glass, praying it'll break into a million pieces. The sounds are not nearly as loud as the cackling of fire behind me, but I hear the crash of plastic and metal on glass like a drum. I follow the pattern over and over. A small crack forms on the surface, and I slam the chair down harder.

The blaze is so close to me that sweat drops down my back, sinking into my shirt. Even though I have a plan, I can't stop the panic seizing my mind.

"C'mon, c'mon, work, work, work! " I chant to myself.

Out of nowhere, the window to my farthest left crashes. It literally splits itself into large pieces, like someone has thrown a boulder at it. When a figure breaks the remaining pieces with his hand, I realize that I might survive after all. I rush at him.

"We have to get out!" I shout.

He has a sweater over his mouth and nose. Glowing eyes blink in response, and Rhys gestures to the broken window.

I crawl through it, not caring that all I have on are thin pajamas in the cold Minnesota night. I balance myself on the thin ledge underneath my window, inching my way to a tree branch, dangling tantalizingly close. I glance back to make sure Rhys is following me, and when his body brushes mine I breathe a sigh of relief. Together, and with painstaking slowness, we move forward, balancing on the thin ledge like tightrope walkers. I look down at the hard ground below, and hesitate. He nudges me onward, his body strong and reliable. When I reach the thick branch I swing my leg over one side, sliding backward until my butt touches the base of the branch. Then I maneuver my body around the trunk of the tree, and shimmy down. The rough surface scratches me, but the cold has already made me numb. When I'm less than two feet off the ground, soft hands touch my back, helping me jump off.

"You okay?" Lenora's wide eyes are glossy in the night sky.

I shiver, the adrenaline still pumping in my veins.

"Is there anyone else in the house?" she asks with worry.

I shake my head.

She moves me to the side, and nods to the figure behind me. "There's no one else in the house. We need water or something, Rhys! Or else the fire will just continue to burn--" She barely finishes before he sprints off through the front entrance.

Smoke continues to pour outside, covering part of the house with fog. I run after him. He hears my footsteps, and turns to catch me in his arms.

He's incredulous. "What are you doing?"

"Helping you help me!"

"Go back. You'll get hurt."

"You can, too," I retort.

"Not me. I'm Golden Eyes."

Is he serious right now!

Lenora grabs me from behind before I can move. "You can't go in, Kenna!" she wails. Her eyes are frantic.

I turn back to Rhys, but he's disappeared into the house. Frustrated, I push past Lenora with more aggression than she expects, and she falls back. I unwind the garden hose. *Please work, please work.* I turn the knob to open the water. Someone above is listening because water sprays out with a gurgle, and I aim it as high as I can, wanting to drench the whole outside of the house. I settle for my bedroom window.

"Here." I shove the hose toward Lenora. Wrapping my legs around the tree, I tell her, "I'm going to climb back up. Hand me the hose when I'm high enough." She looks ready to argue, but she doesn't, and dutifully does what I ask once I'm back on the branch.

When the firefighters finally arrive, there isn't much to do. We had already contained the fire, and Rhys emerges with dirt and smoke on his face and hands, still looking like a million bucks. I'm embarrassed I notice, and push the thought away.

"Are you okay?" I ask him, thankful and I'm relieved for what he's done.

He nods. "Yeah. You?"

I nod back. I'm suddenly aware I'm dressed in an Angry Bird shirt and a matching pajama pant. I tell myself they probably don't even know who Angry Bird is, so I shouldn't feel too mortified.

"How'd you find me?" I ask. He looks uncomfortable. Belatedly, I realize I just insinuated he was searching for me. *As if he has a reason to,* I remind myself.

"We were at our head-" He stops. "Head *work* place a block from here." He gestures behind us. "We drove by and saw a fire."

"You work this late into the night?" That explains why his eyes always storm whenever I mention work.

"Yes."

"Where are your parents?" Lenora asks. "We should probably let them know."

I rub my forehead. "I'll let Dad know when he comes home." I had to. He'll notice the black soot marks covering part of the house. Not to mention a broken window and a half, and a burnt bedroom.

Neighbors come to ask how I am, but Rhys and Lenora don't leave my side. Maybe they notice the numbness slowly choking me every time I look at my house. I know how close to death I was. I relieved, but I can't stop my teeth from chattering and my body from shaking. Abruptly, vomit rises up my throat, and without warning I run. I hear footsteps behind me, but I don't slow down. When I'm behind a tree, I pour out everything inside me: terror, fear, and my relief I've survived. It tastes like chicken and processed cheese.

A hand pulls my hair back, and it's gentle, rubbing soft circles around my back. "Easy," Rhys whispers. "It's ok," he says. I shake my head. Doesn't he realize what could've happened?

"My dad can't live without me."

"He doesn't have to," Rhys says.

I don't notice I've spoken out loud until Rhys answered. My shaking has dwindled, but his hands don't leave, and they continue to stroke my back.

"I'll always be here. I'm not going to let you die," he says. I look up. "I've done a pretty good job of saving you so far, haven't I?" He grins. "I *am* Golden Eyes after all."

Even though I'm still anxious from the fire, I'm slowly melting inside from his smile. *You save everyone,* I think tenderly. Out loud I say, "Eh. Superman would've gotten here faster."

"I doubt it. I can beam pretty quick."

Remembering how he saved me from the truck yesterday morning, I ask, "How did you save me from the truck so fast yesterday?"

"Some of us can move a little faster than humans."

"I'd say *a lot* faster." His small smile tells me I'm probably right.

"Isn't it human custom to thank the person who saves your life?" he suddenly asks.

"Thank you."

I'm so close to him I can feel the heat from his body. His hands are still rubbing circles on my back, and the soothing motion has the opposite effect he's intending it for. My heart accelerates, pounding harder. I notice something small and black on his face. Debris maybe? I resist the urge to touch him and wipe it off.

"It's not safe here anymore, Kenna."

My stomach plummets. Last night I'd watched a report on World News Tonight about a religious group who vowed to kill every Saguinox on Earth. When questioned by Diane Sawyer, their representative responded aliens on earth are unnatural. God created each of us for different worlds, and we shouldn't mix. When Diane asked for a response from her T.V. audience, someone immediately twittered: God shouldn't have given aliens the intelligence to build space traveling ships then. #insteadofhatingweshouldgetsmarter.

Gazing into Rhys's worried face, I wonder what he's hiding. Has there been an investigation about the incident yesterday? Is it part of a larger conspiracy? "Do you and Lenora have to leave?"

He hesitates. "Sort of."

What does that mean?

His hands find mine, and my fingers curl around his. It feels so good, and I hold on even when the static shocks us. We ride out the small bolt before he takes a breath, making a decision.

"Come on." He says it with such authority that I follow him. When we get back to Lenora she's waiting next to her expensive car. She seems nervous.

"Ready?" she asks.

"For what?" I'm confused. But I don't think she's talking to me.

She moves closer until she is inches from my body, and the glow in her eyes brightens. Violet spots glare, growing luminous.

I suck in a breath, staring at the dizzying lullaby. Her smile is angelic, and I can't help the grin fluttering on my lips.

"Get in the car, Kenna."

I do as she says because I can't bare not to. Something in my mind is rumbling. I rub my hands on the smooth leather interior. I want to sleep on it. They've closed the door, but her voice drifts into my ears from outside.

"I'm not sure I can do it," I hear her confess.

"It's okay if you're nervous. Turn it on as long as you can," Rhys instructs her. "Can you do it?"

"Okay."

A second later Rhys slides next to me, and I realize I'm cold. I reach for him, and he lets me hold his hand for a moment. He squeezes my fingers, then he's fumbling

with something, and I'm suddenly afraid to look. Warning bells sound in my head, and I know this isn't a good
idea. I open my mouth to protest. Lenora is behind the
wheel, and turns toward me.

"Kenna." Her irises are all purple now, and she's calm-
ing me down because my whole body becomes limp. I
start to panic. My eyes refuse to leave hers though, and
mauve colors dance in front of me swaying like seaweed
on an ocean floor. "Time to go," she whispers. Her voice
is hypnotizing, and I blink.

I'm frozen, and when Rhys sticks a needle into my
vein, I realize I've made a big mistake.

Chapter 11

When I awake darkness is all I see and I'm afraid until I remember what happened; then I am terrified. I try to make a sound, but I can't. My throat isn't working, and gurgling gasps are all I can muster. I'm blindfolded, and my hands are crossed in front of me, held together with a rope that bites my skin. I'm moving, but my legs aren't carrying me. Someone else is. I hear a strong heartbeat against my ear, and I concentrate on it to help me keep calm.

The wind is harsh and loud. Someone's put a blanket over me. I smell a feminine hint of lilac, and I wonder if Lenora is close by. *Lenora*. She did something to me, I'm sure of it. My mind replays every moment I spent in their company, but there isn't much to go through. I panic as I think about what the Saguinox might do with me. Eat me? Torture me? Bring back to their planet for some sick experiment? All the thoughts running in my head fill me with anger and nausea, and I wonder if I'm going to throw up again.

"That way," a soft voice whispers. Lenora is next to us.

I think of her easy charm, and beautiful face and I want to kick myself. Why did I agree to go in the car with her? Why did I follow Rhys? Why had I been so dumb? They're *aliens* for god's sake! They don't even have the same anatomy as me. But deep inside I know why I followed Rhys, why I want to follow him: he sees me when others can't. He saves me when I can't save myself.

I'm humiliated.

Rhys was all an act, as fake as the Golden Eyes hero I'd made in my head.

I want to punch him, but I settle for thrashing my shoulder into his large chest instead. He doesn't acknowledge it, doesn't even flinch. That only makes me madder. Images of what I want to do to him flash in my mind: kicking him in the shins, hitting him with a shovel, flipping him on his back with ferocity the way I've seen a WWE wrestler do once.

I don't stop hitting him with my shoulder, and I hope my actions tell him something about me. His words about me being a survivor come back in my head. *You're.* Hit. *Damn.* Hit. *Right!* Hit. He only holds me tighter, and I'm not sure what that gesture means.

When I exhaust myself, I rest my head on the chest I've worked so hard to hurt. I'm still weak. Whatever they gave me was powerful. I wonder if it's human made.

I listen for clues about where I am. I know I'm away from the city because I can't hear cars or people. All I hear are owls, and the rustle of trees and leaves. If I strain my ears I think I can even hear the sounds of waves crashing, but whatever they shot me up with makes it hurt to focus too long. The sound of something opening alerts me. We've arrived, and I stiffen in his arms. Something small and pointy nudges my skin.

"No." Rhys voice sounds strained, like something's hurting him. I wonder if it's me, and I can't help the smug smile tugging at my lips.

"What if she fights?" Lenora asks.

"It will be all right," he says quietly, gently.

"I don't know, Rhys." Lenora sounds uncertain. "She doesn't seem like she'll come quietly." *Smart girl,* I snarl silently. *Now if only you can come closer so I can claw your eyes out!* I must've made a sound because Rhys's arms tighten.

"I'll take care of it," he says.

"We have to undress her and put the offering on," Lenora says, amused. "And I don't think *you* should be doing that."

Rhys makes a sound, and it sounds suspiciously like a smirk. "I'm sure I can figure it out."

More images of things I want to do to him enter my mind, including using the ropes on my hands to tie him to a tree for the wolves.

"How about this, you can get the offering on her and I'll be close by in case you need my... skills." Rhys suggests.

"All right," she reluctantly agrees. "If she wakes up the whole compound with her screaming, don't tell me I didn't warn you."

"She won't."

"If she tries to run, don't tell me I-"

"She won't." There's a pause. "Don't you trust me?" Rhys asks softly.

"You know I do," Lenora replies just as softly. "But Malachi-"

"Shh!" he hisses, and I know he doesn't want to say more in front of me. "Let's go."

My legs stir, and I try to stretch them, testing them without him noticing. I'm scared he does though, because he walks faster. I can hear Lenora's heels clicking softly, and I know we're inside a building. A few more doors open, and then we stop. He settles my body onto something hard.

A chair.

I try to sit, but my body's slouching like my bones have disappeared. A gentle hand hoists me back up, tenderly laying my neck back. I'm facing the ceiling and faint light penetrates through the cloth over my eyes. Lenora's clicking fades away, and we're alone.

"I know you can hear me," Rhys says in a low voice. "Just do everything you're told and you'll be ok. Nod if you understand."

Bastard, I try to say, but nothing comes out.

"Nod if you understand." Maybe he senses my fear because his voice is gentler. "Lenora's going to undress you. She's going to put you in something else. Please don't try to leave or they will send someone to get you. There are consequences for prisoners who try to escape."

Prisoners? My throat feels dry. What did he mean by that? Why was I in prison? My questions can't be voiced, and he won't answer them anyway so I keep the growing terror to myself.

His hands touch my shoulders, and I'm surprised. I wonder if he knows they're shaking. "Please don't leave, Kenna," he repeats softly.

I don't answer him. I couldn't if I wanted to anyway.

"I'll wait by the door," he informs Lenora. "She's alert."

I hear her walking, approaching me with hesitation. "I think you have to keep your blindfolds on. So I'm just going to help you pull your shirt and pants off, okay?" She lifts my shirt up, but it's hard because my hands are still tied in front of me. Lenora pauses. "I wonder if I should cut the ropes off.'

Yes, yes, my mind is screaming. *Do it!*

She asks Rhys, and his quick "no" seals the deal. She goes back to struggling with the thin shirt, and I hear a tear as she finally pulls it over my arms and head.

"I'm sorry!" Lenora sounds apologetic. "I hope you didn't like that shirt. There is a... very cute bird on it." She sounds so contrite I'm almost amused, but then I remember how I got here and I hate her again. "There are many birds on your pants though. I'll be careful, I promise."

The pants are easier, partly because my legs feel like putty she can move any which way she likes. Within seconds I have on nothing but a bra and panty.

"Don't peek, Rhys!" she calls out.

"I'm not," he responds, but he sounds like he's laughing, and I get madder.

She puts something soft and silky over my head. It smells fresh, like clean linen. Struggling, she calls out, "Rhys! I have to cut the ropes. I can't get the dress on."

He sighs and walks over.

I'm mortified. Even though the top part of me is covered, my thighs and legs are not.

"Pull off the dress," he tells her.

I make a loud strangled sound, the loudest I've made yet, and they pause. Rhys comes closer and whispers to me, "I won't look. I promise. Do you trust me?"

Hell no! I shout in my head.

The words still can't come, but he knows what I'm thinking because he's saying, "Use this pocket knife to cut it off. I'll stand behind you in case she tries something." His voice gets dramatically loud to make sure I hear. "I'm turning my back, Kenna, *I won't see a thing.*" All I can think about is I wish my legs could kick.

When the ropes finally come off, I make a sound of relief. I want to rub my wrists, but I have to stretch my fingers and arms. It's hard to raise my arms without help, but I try anyway.

"Good," Lenora says encouragingly. "Just keep stretching them." I'm confused. Ten minutes ago she wanted to knock me out with a needle, but now she's encouraging me to regain my strength back? It makes no sense, but I can't think anymore because she's pulling the dress over me again. This time it flows down without a hitch.

Lenora adjusts my top until I'm properly covered, then says, "Ok, Rhys, all done."

All I hear is a sharp intake of breath. There is silence for a long moment and I'm wondering what he sees.

"I'll take her to her room," he finally says, his voice thick and strained with something that makes my insides warm. His arms are gentle when he picks me up.

I want to squirm with frustration. I want to hate him so bad. I *do* hate him, but he plays with my emotions when he touches me like I'm something precious. He pulls my head closer onto his chest. His breath is warm on my forehead, and I'm tingly there. Something sounding like metal opening drifts into my ears, and I brace myself.

He sets me down on the hard floor. "When your hands are back to normal you can take your blindfold off."

I try to speak, but only disjointed sounds form.

"You'll be able to talk in an hour or two," he says. "You might not see me much. Do what you're told, but *listen to your instincts.*" He touches the side of my head. "Listen to the voices in here."

There's a long moment of quiet where I can't hear anything but his breathing. In the darkness, my sense of touch is heightened. The barest whisper of his fingers trace the sides of my face. Against my will, I shiver. For some sick reason I want this moment to last forever. My body repulses me. Within seconds, he's gone, his strong footsteps fading as more terror grows inside me.

I'm more scared alone than when I was with Lenora and Rhys. Feelings of confusion and betrayal flow through me. For a long while, I remain motionless, willing myself not to cry. I lay my head down, but don't close my eyes. It's still dark either way.

Out of boredom and adrenaline-filled fear, I stretch my body and attempt to move it. My legs are sluggish, but my arms are coming around. It takes time, but eventually I can lift them. Soon my fingers can move with enough coordination. I'm able to rip the cloth from my eyes. More darkness greets me. With enough concentration my eyes adjust, and that's when I see where I am- *what* I'm in.

He was right. I'm a prisoner. And Rhys had locked me in a cell with no way to get out.

CHAPTER 12

I hear the screams first.

At first I think it's a nightmare. I see the dingy walls surrounding me, and the foreboding metal door, and I know this is no dream. The cell is archaic with only a hole for a toilet. There's no bed and no blankets. The floor is even and smooth, but it's cold and uncomfortable.

The voice screams again, louder this time, and I jump up. There's a small rectangular window in the door, and I stand on my tiptoes to peek through.

Someone is dragging a girl by her hair. They move past us and I gasp. She's wearing the same scarlet colored dress I have on. What does it mean? Do people wearing red die first? I watch them until they round a corner, and the last thing I see are the ends of her ruby dress flittering helplessly in the wind.

I step back, numb with fear. All at once understanding comes at me full force. I'm alone. No one knows where I am. I don't even know where I am. No way to get in. No way to get out. Trapped, and at the utter mercy of aliens.

I start hyperventilating, something I've never done before, but the short breaths keep coming, smaller each time. My chest constricts because I'm fighting to take in enough oxygen, but it's not enough, and I'm shaking so badly. I curl into a ball, covering my face with my arms. No one can see the tears glistening in my eyes. No one hears my sob over my harsh breathing. And, even as I lay on the cold floor, looking defeated, I know I can't be.

I have to get out.

I have to tell everyone the truth.

The Saguinox are not what they seem.

Shame covers me, making my body hot with anger. How the aliens must've laughed, seeing how malleable we were. Humans welcomed them with open arms like the baby life forms they thought we were.

My humiliation is mixed with guilt. Every lustful thought I ever had about Rhys runs in my head, bulldozing my conscience and crumbling my heart. I literally handed myself to them tonight, tricked by a pair of Angel eyes and a handsome face that's poison.

My anger's the only thing that gets me through the night.

Chapter 13

An alarm rings, screeching through dreams of glowing eyes and fire. I jerk awake, and notice that I'm still in the same position from the night before. I stretch my neck, arms and legs, feeling lighter as I realize my body is back in working order. The alarm sounds again, and the buzzing hurts my ears. *There is a loudspeaker in the room somewhere.* I stand.

Walking, I peer through the door. I try to look for faces, but the windows are small, and the lights dim. I see nothing but an empty corridor with gray walls. It reminds me of a nightmare I had, and goose bumps ripple over my arms.

"All clear."

Someone's walking, and I press my face against the glass to see. He has dark hair and eyes, and his lips are turned in a frown. There are two other men with him. All three look ahead, their glowing eyes a beacon in the dark. He nods, and the sounds of opening doors rumble in the corridor. I step back as the door of my own personal prison push out. My hands tighten on the handle, and with a shaky breath I shove the door forward, stepping out.

When I'm in the corridor I see there are about a dozen people standing with me. I gasp. I'm wrong. There are a dozen people and *other creatures* standing with me.

My eyes are wide. I can't help but stare at the one closest to me. Her skin is green, completely and vibrantly green. Her black irises are large and luminous. Her body is shaped like a human girl, but scales that cover her chest, belly, and crotch. A tail hangs behind her, and I only notice it because she swings it, sweeping it to the front. Her feet have toes, but they're oval shaped, and are like green raindrops. She's not wearing a dress, but a red shawl covers her. It's the same color as mine, and she pushes the hood over her face. She turns to the Saguinox, and I do, too.

"You will be fed this morning, and then you will return to the caves to harvest. Tomorrow some of you will offer yourselves to the crystal." There is a collective sound of horror, and I look around, afraid. He is unperturbed. "Do as you're told. Escape is an illusion. Should you try," -a malicious smile appears on his face- "he *will* find you."

I'm not sure who "he" is, but the alarm on every person's face makes me not want to find out.

As suddenly as he comes, he leaves, and the people to my left turn. I follow knowing that my survival depends on my ability to blend in.

We march like soldiers, each behind the other, heads bowed. The corners of my eyes scan my new surroundings, taking note of the nightmare I've suddenly found myself in. We join other rows of people, all dressed in scarlet red. Even though it's hard to see, I put the pieces together like a puzzle. Cells line either side of me, and I know there's more than one level because I can hear the same monotone footsteps echoing above. It looks exactly like what I'd imagine a prison to look like, but instead of white walls, gray is the color most used. We pass by what I assume are guards, though they're dressed casually in shirts and jeans. They're probably dressed that way to blend in when they leave the prison. Anything less might cause suspicion.

Glowing eyes watch us. Each gaze is filled with disgust, and their thoughts are reflected on their faces: we are inferior. They're the superior.

A few Saguinox hold weapons like guns and daggers, but the majority don't. They don't have to. The warning is palpable, even to me: obey or else.

I feel like a lamb, moving toward her slaughter. We enter into a cafeteria -like space. The tables are placed in straight rows. They're cafeteria tables, but metal handcuffs are attached to the center of each. I can smell food, but instead of making me hungry, it has the opposite affect and I want to vomit.

We're herded into two lines. They give us wooden bowls and a spoon, and watching the others, I kneel to receive the meager portion. The silence is delicate, and I try desperately to quiet my stomping, but my fear seems to have made my feet louder. My only consolation is that, like everywhere else, everyone here ignores me. They

106 · MARI ARDEN

don't hear my feet. Or maybe they do, but they just don't care.

I follow the person ahead of me to my seat. There are guards around, but no one moves to handcuff us. Instead, the prisoners do it themselves. I observe the girl beside me adjusting one handcuff over her left hand. I feel sick, watching her. What kind of perverted game is this? They're forcing us to confine our bodies, to do the one thing we're desperate *not* to do.

I slide in next to her, and repeat her motions. When the cuffs click onto my wrist, I fight back the urge to take it off. I want to throw the restraint against the wall, and break it into a million pieces. *I need to blend in,* I remind myself, taking a deep breath.

The anger is boiling underneath me, but I try to ignore it. I take a bite of the cream-colored soup, and gag. I clench the table in an effort to force it down, and it works even though my stomach is heaving. The creature from before notices me, and she pauses, catching my eye. She demonstrates taking little sips at a time. No one notices my outburst, except her and I follow her motions, taking tiny sips. The herbal taste is more bearable in bits, but she's sipping fast. Maybe I need to, too.

Soon another bell rings. No one moves, though. Slowly the guards move between us, taking their sweet time, showing us how insignificant we truly are. I watch as one guard unlocks the metal handcuff of the girl beside me. When it's my turn, I hold my breath in anticipation. When the metal opens, falling back from my wrist, I bite back a gasp. My hands feel lighter.

We take our bowls to the other side of the room, and hand them to other scarlet clad workers. There is no eye contact, and when my finger accidently touches the worker's, she shrinks back.

I continue to follow the person in front of me, but the two rows are closer together. The creature from before is next to me, and her tail lightly touches my calf. I pause for a millisecond before moving.

"You blend in very well," she whispers. Her voice is thick with a European sounding accent. "It's hard to notice you."

I decide to be honest. "It's sort of a trick of mine."

"Oh." She grins. "It's a nice trick to have."

I don't say anything.

"My name is Chloris."

"I'm Kenna," I murmur.

"I'll show you what to do when we get to the caves," she offers.

"Thanks."

When we step outside, I'm greeted with a rush of cold air that sweeps the folds of my dress between my legs. If they notice the cold, no one shows it and we move as silent as ghosts. In the distance I can see trees and hills. I hear the wired fence around us, buzzing with electricity, and it's so cold I want to move closer. Soon I see a cave up ahead, its mouth stretching high above us. I want to see more, but my head remains bowed, submissive.

Good girl, the thought whispers in my mind, and I almost stumble. I clutch the red fabric of my dress in my palms so I won't trip. My heart's racing. Had a guard just talked to me in my head? Head low, I search around. All I see are scarlet folds and shuffling feet. Anger, desperation, and terror pulse through me, shooting panic through my body. What sorts of powers do the Saguinox have? Suddenly, I remember Lenora's eyes, and the tingling in my head. I wonder if she's done something to me. Has she opened my brain up to the other Saguinox?

I try to listen again, but the voice is gone.

We travel further into the cave until the only light available are torches and candles that burn dimmer than embers. Even the color from our red dresses has faded, vanishing as shadowed veils.

As if she senses my thoughts, Chloris whispers, "You'll get used to it."

I'm afraid I won't because the further we go in, the less I feel of myself. Darkness is all around us, and my thoughts are evaporating into air. Soon I think nothing, feel nothing, see nothing, but black shadows all around.

I don't know we've stopped until I bump into the person in front of me. She doesn't acknowledge what I do, so I don't say sorry. We're moving slow, and I wonder why. Someone is handing out helmets with a light attached. It's weak, but it's better than nothing. Putting it on, I'm grateful when the faint beam flashes ahead. We keep walking, and I'm suddenly glad I ate the disgusting soup from this morning because I have a suspicion what we'll be doing in this cave is work.

We start going down on a slope, then we walk down a flight of stairs. It's as dark as before so I don't know if we're underground. The silence is deafening, and I want to turn back so bad. I don't, and even though my mind is afraid, my body isn't, and it keeps moving even when I'm too scared to. We keep walking and walking and when we finally stop, I'm a little breathless. I don't doubt we're miles from the cave entrance.

A pair of glowing eyes light up a feminine face, and she stands on a chair above us. The light on her helmet is a little brighter, and she aims it over our heads. "*This* is what we are looking for." She holds something small between her fingers, but no matter how my eyes strain I can't see it. "If you are new, raise your hand and I will come closer so you can see it." She pauses, but no hands rise.

Chloris's tail touches my ankles, and she shakes her head.

I already know. *I'm not dumb enough to declare myself a newbie,* I say with my eyes. I'd be fresh meat for those bastards.

"Crystals," Chloris murmurs so softly I almost think I imagine it.

"This cave is vast. This area is rich with Braxi. It should not be hard to find." She pauses, staring hard at us. "You only have to *dig* for it." She throws a shovel to the person in front of her, and she falls, knocking down the person behind her. The Saguinox female makes an annoyed sound and jumps down. Her hand lashes out. The slap echoes around us, followed by desperate weeping and begging.

"Get up," she snarls. "I have no time to waste on your useless human tears!" She slaps the girl again, and we jump back, making room for her to come through. Her hand brushes against mine as she moves by, and I feel a chill that has nothing to do with the cave temperature.

"The shovels are up ahead," Chloris informs me when the Saguinox footsteps can no longer be heard. She shows me the way. The tools are dirty and smelly, but I know better than to complain. There are a few guards with us, but they don't seem too alert. There are more than fifty prisoners down here, and only a handful of Saguinox, yet they are unafraid. One is dozing off as I walk by. *Why don't we revolt?* I think. *The odds are in our favor.* I turn back to where we got the shovels. From where I'm at I can see carts and carts full of shovels, brushes, wedges and sledgehammers. Suddenly, I feel something inside; it's pounding beneath my skin.

"I want the sledgehammer," I say to Chloris.

She looks at me like I'm crazy. "We're looking for *crystals*, Kenna, not breaking a wall. Trust me, shovels are best."

I don't say more because I need time to think through what I want to do. I'm so close behind her I have to be careful not to step on her tail. "Chloris."

"Hmm?" She's maneuvering around the other prisoners, going in deeper.

I hesitate for just a moment. "If you don't mind me asking, what are you?"

"Shape shifter."

This time I stumble behind her, falling onto my knees. Unfortunately, there's also a rock underneath me, and the edge connects with my bone. I hiss, but don't make a loud enough sound to catch the guard's attention.

"Kenna! Are you okay?" She sounds anxious. I rub my knee.

"Just... not expecting that."

She gives me a smile, and her eyes are gentle. "There's a lot humans don' t know about."

I'm reminded of Lenora's conversation with me earlier. *You're just a baby planet,* she'd said.

"Yeah, I'm learning that."

She helps me up. Her hand is like mine, but green and with longer nails.

"Do you come from a different planet, too?" I ask, wiping my bottom.

"My ancestors a long time ago, probably. But I'm an earthling like you, born and raised." She has my shovel in her hands, and she hands it back. "Come on."

She's moving, but I'm rooted to the floor, stunned. She'd been *born and raised* here? How's that possible? How many others are out there?

"Are there more like you?" I whisper.

"Some like me. Some not."

My mind's racing with questions. Her words echo in my brain. *Some like me. Some not.* What does that mean? Is she referring to different species of aliens? Is she the good guy, and the others are bad? More importantly, can I trust her? Chloris turns back, waiting for me to catch up.

Do I follow?

I look around at the other prisoners whose gaze refuse to touch mine. I turn back to Chloris. Her eyes are curious.

She's the only one willing to help.

I don't have a choice. Not really. Not if I want to escape.

Chloris takes me to a spot more secluded from the others, and shows me how to dig.

"The Braxi crystals are small and white. Try to dig without cracking them. They're no use broken or cracked. They need to be perfect." She demonstrates, shoveling a handful of dirt each time. She's careful to not push too hard, and wiggles the tool, rather than pushing it in. I imitate her, but it isn't natural. The shovel is so heavy I want to use its weight to push down, but I have to resist, and use my arms to make it light. She has to crouch every few minutes, and use her hands and the light on her helmet to search for the small crystals. It takes a long time, but when she finally gets one, she shows me. I adjust the light, and stare in awe at the perfect white crystal. It's oval shaped, and glitters. I take it in my hand. It feels warm. I make a fist around it, and when I feel something, my eyes shoot up to Chloris.

"It's *vibrating*," I breathe.

"They're used to store energy and magic," she informs. A small smile lights up her face. "Beautiful, isn't it?"

I'm in shock, but I agree. Shape shifters? Crystals that store magic? "How has all of this stayed *hidden*?" I don't just mean the crystals and she seems to understand that.

"Humans see and hear what they want to see and hear. Arrogance can make you blind."

Still bewildered, I shake my head. My fists close around the Braxi again to feel the pleasant sensation. "What do they need these crystals for?"

"Evil." She says it quietly, but with such sadness I'm speechless.

The Saguinox don't mean to join us.

"They mean to conquer us." My whispered realization is met with silence.

Chloris and I stare at each other. Her eyes are large and sad. Hopeless.

Discouraged, we don't talk anymore. For a long time there is only silence as we work. She demonstrates how to use the shovels to dig the cave walls. My stomach is rumbling, and I'm thirsty. Chloris takes me to a small water stand and a worker hands me a little cup.

"Don't drink too much," she warns me. "There's nowhere to relieve yourself." I'm angry when I drink. "We're just animals to them." I watch a guard as he casually leans on a worker, using her head to lean on.

"Yes," Chloris affirms.

I turn angrily to her. "How can you just accept this?"

Her eyes are wide, and she sneaks a glance at the worker before shaking her head. I bite my lip. "Come on." She gestures and we go back to our stations.

I try to talk, but she doesn't want to anymore. I rebuke myself for letting my true feelings come through. I need her to give me information. I find the sledgehammers and shovels. I dare not stare at them too long, but my heart is racing with determination again. I can't stop myself from getting closer.

"Switching shovels," I murmur to Chloris, and leave before she can argue. It doesn't feel right, but I try to soften my loud feet. That doesn't work, and I'm thankful that like in the real world, no one seems to notice me much here. *I hope Chloris won't notice how long I'm gone.*

I'm the only one near the sledgehammers, and I pick one up, feeling the weight of it in my hands. I admire the rusty metal head, and a certain handsome face with glowing eyes flitters in my head. *Yes, this will work* just *fine.*

I clutch it tightly in my hand and casually walk forward, away from Chloris and the other workers. I try to move slowly so as not to arouse suspicion. I move past more prisoners, their scarlet attire more visible with their helmet lights. For the first time, I wonder what the red dress means. Rhys and Lenora had referred to it as "the offering". *Maybe the Saguinox have some ritual where people are "offered" to an alien god.* It doesn't sound far-fetched, and feeling a deep apprehension, I keep walking.

The slope is moving upward, and there are no workers beyond this point. It's careless to keep going so I stop. I dig, using the sledgehammer and my hands. *I should've brought the shovel too,* I think. My heart's dancing wildly in my chest. *Please stay invisible, please stay invisible.*

It takes time, but I finally get it. The hole is big and deep enough to hide a sledgehammer. I glance around, careful to look nonchalant. When I'm sure no one is watching I shove it in, and frantically cover the sledgehammer with hardened dirt, and any other materials I can find. I take in air, and it smells like dirt and metal. I'm so busy breathing I don't notice the body until my head connects with an elbow. I gasp, turn around, and instantly fall back.

Her glowing eyes are cold, and scrunched in anger. I can't help but stare back with wide eye panic.

"Where did *you* come from?" she snarls. Her short hair is spiked up like a boy's, and she's looking menacingly at me. "Answer me."

"I-I..." For a second my mind is blank. She looks so threatening and so terrifying that my mind is frozen. I can't feel the sledgehammer underneath me, but my heart's beating violently.

"Don't you know how to talk?" She wrinkles her nose. "You're not one of those mute humans, are you?"

I shake my head. "No."

Suddenly her hands lash out, and she has the back of my head. She carries half my body off the ground, pulling painfully at my hair. "Don't think I didn't notice you here by yourself. Did you think you would get away with that?"

I can't talk. I can't breathe, and she jerks me to my feet. "Lazy scum. You humans are the worst." She pulls me by my hair, dragging me like a bag so hard I cry out. I'm pushed against something hard. The metal tub connects with my shoulder blade, and my skin instantly tears. The pain burns.

Out of nowhere I see a flame in my mind. It's exquisite, and it's swaying gently, ready to go where I need it to go.

I know exactly where it needs to shoot, but before I can, a voice shouts in my head.

No! The voice sounds alarmed. *No flames, take it out!*

I shriek.

The voice is back in my head.

Something hard is shoved into my arms. A shovel.

"Everyone works in the caves," the Saguinox guard informs me coldly. "You're no exception. If I catch you slacking off again, you'll be given to the crystal. Do you understand?" She pushes me back. "Do you?"

I nod, but I don't look at her. I'm shaking. My mind feels numb, like something heavy's inside. I'm so focused inside myself that I can't look at her. She takes it as a sign of submission. I wait, and even when the sound of her footsteps has disappeared, I can't move. My insides feel jumpy, and I'm anxious, and tense and fearful, and all of it twists in my gut like a cyclone.

I'm trembling so bad I don't notice the smell of burning metal underneath my fingers until my eyes sting from the smoke.

I drop the shovel and jump back.

It's smoldering.

* * *

It's dark when we're allowed back outside. My back aches, and I'm glad to walk with my head low, because it hurts to straighten my body. Supper is comprised of the same disgusting soup. It tastes like what I'd imagine liquid roots would taste like. Even though I'm starving my hunger isn't enough to drown out the revolting taste, so I sip at it, each mouthful worse than the last.

Chloris is ignoring me, although I catch her shooting me an empathetic look when she hears me gag on the food. No one talks. No one moves unless told to, and I actually feel relieved to go back my cell.

When the door closes blackness envelope me. I try to sleep, but pictures of my parents churn in my mind like a broken movie. I miss my dad, and if I breathe deeply enough I can smell past the perfume of alcohol on his clothes, to the woodsy scent of his skin. I wonder if he's searching for me. When I think about how lost he must be, I feel a hot rage inside, and it's all I can do to not pound against the walls, screaming. But I don't want to give them the satisfaction of seeing me do that, so I pull my knees to my chest instead.

My mind wanders back to what happened in the caves earlier, but I shut my eyes, refusing to acknowledge it. I'm so cold, and a memory of mom, dad and I sipping hot chocolate during a wintry night drifts into my mind. I remember the warmth, and I sigh, pretending that it's here. I hear the fireplace in my head. I see the dark orange blaze, twirling like dancers over and under the logs. The flames bend, swinging in a contained space and I imagine touching it, feeling it through my body...

I fall asleep with the flames brushing my face, feeling more alone than ever. As I drift into unconsciousness, the tender promise whispers inside my head. *I'll always be here.*

Chapter 14

When the alarm sounds, I jump, panicked. The first things I see are the windowless walls of my prison. Lifting myself up, I notice something strange. The floor is burnt. *What the-*

"All clear."

The door opens, and it's my cue to step forward. I can't move, staring at a large black spot where my face had been. Reaching out, my fingers brush against the hot surface. I jerk back when I feel the heat. Frantic, I look around to see if anyone's noticed. I can see scarlet dresses through the wide crack in the door. I don't have anymore time. Quickly, I stand, and move to join the group.

My eyes find Chloris. Maybe she sees something in my face because she gives me a small smile. I shake my head.

The three men from yesterday morning are back. The speaker begins the same way. "You will be fed this morning, and then you will return to the caves to harvest. Yesterday's batch was pathetic. We are expecting better today." He pauses, smiling, but it's not really a smile and everyone is nervous. No one will look at each other. He continues, "Do as you're told. Escape is an illusion. Should you attempt, he will find you, and you will be very, very sorry." The last part is said with such softness it sounds more like breaths than words.

Chloris looks scared. I feel sick.

The alien begins to walk, taking a few steps before stopping before the first prisoner. Out of the corner of my eye, I see the girl in front of him is trembling, and his finger gently pushes her chin up. He stares at her for a long moment, and the tension is unbearable.

"Go," he finally whispers, and her sigh of relief is palpable.

He walks to the next prisoner, a man. He repeats the same process, holding his chin roughly. His red robe covers his body completely, but his arms are bare. The seconds tick by slowly before he says, "Go."

Another ripple of relief.

Like the others, the one after the male is also a human, a girl. His hands go to her neck, tracing shapes with his thumb. His eyes rake her body, examining for signs of what? Sickness? Disease? He whispers one word close to her ear, but says it loud enough so we can all hear. "Stay."

Instantly, her anguish fills the corridor, and she's begging, "Please! No! Don't take me to the crystal. I can do better. I-"

He squeezes her neck, choking her with force.

She sputters, begging for air, but it's useless.

"Did I say you can speak?" he thunders. "Did I?" His

face is red with fury, and I forget to bow my head.

I look up, taking a step forward, needing to do something.

Chloris' soft squeak enters my brain at the last second, and her eyes are abnormally wide, telling me to stay put.

I feel strange. My mind is humming, buzzing with something strong. I feel it gathering around me.

Stop. I'm so surprised by the voice I *do* stop. *Don't move.*

I'm motionless.

Survive. Stay alive, it continues.

I nearly choke with shock because the voice is distinctly male with a familiar low timbre, tickling my mind. *I'm going crazy!* I think with dizzying fear.

The Saguinox guard shoves the human girl to the floor, and she's weeping uncontrollably. She doesn't speak, but she crawls to him, grasping his knees with pitiful sobs. He looks disgusted and he spits on her. "Lock her in the cell until they come."

"No! Please!" She's being dragged back into the room, and when the door shuts, her screams are no longer heard. There's complete stillness as he continues the selection. With each passing "go", I become more nervous, too scared to talk to myself, not wanting the crazy to come out now, when I need my sanity the most.

The girl chosen to stay had looked healthy. Anxiety knots are in my stomach because the selection seems to be random. That knowledge frightens me.

When the guard is next to me, I almost stop breathing. "Stay," he announces to the girl beside me. Her tears sound weak, and heaviness grips my heart. This close I hear how sick she is, and I know nothing can help her. She's dragged back inside her cell, but her screams have already faded to coughs.

He moves like he's going to go past me, but then his feet hit mine, and I almost kick myself. *Move back into formation!* my mind screeches. But it's too late, I've made myself known, and the Saguinox guard is a breath away from my body. I hear the groan in my brain, and it doesn't come from me.

His glowing eyes look down me, slowly coming up. I straighten, trying to look healthy, but not really sure if that's what he's looking for. I strain to look submissive. He watches me for a long moment. Eyes downcast, I see his hands lift up to touch me. When his fingers brush my chin to raise my eyes, I hear a roar of panic in my head, and-

Static booms over a speaker, and he drops his hand, covering his ears. The high pitch sound breaks in and out. "Bloody hell," he snaps, glancing at the speaker attached to a wall just below the ceiling. Sounds from the loudspeaker continue to be indiscernible, and he barks, "Go check what that's about. Damn machines."

One of the men walks off to obey, and I hold my breath. Squeezing my eyes shut, I stop breathing. Almost in slow motion, I hear the rustle of clothes moving, and low cuss words. Then I shake with relief when I hear him pass. *Close call.*

Hardly! is the clipped reply inside my head.

Three are chosen to stay, and the rest of us go. The

mood is bleaker than I've ever felt, and I have no trouble bowing my head, staring with misery at our shuffling feet. Out of the corner of my eye, I see the hairy ends of a green tail, and Chloris whispers, "You okay?"

"Yes. Just traumatized, and afraid of some dumb crystal I know nothing about." I shake my head.

"You don't want to know," she tells me. "There are no words."

I don't question her because she knows more about all of this than I do. I'm moving a little slower than yesterday due to newfound aches and pains. The guards watch us coolly, and their stares unnerve me.

Chloris catches me looking at our captors. "Those are the guards."

"I figured that."

"No," she shakes her head. "The Saguinox have a hierarchy. The guards are on the bottom. They do the job no one else wants to do."

We're *the job no one else wants to do?* I'm angry.

"There is no honor in watching prisoners," Chloris continues. "That's why there are so few guards. None of them want to be here, but none of them have a way out. It's kind of like a caste system. Once they've been identified as a guard, they will remain a guard forever. To the Saguinox there is only honor in fighting. They value their warriors above everyone else."

"Warriors?"

"Killers," she clarifies.

My stomach drops. "Where are the warriors?" Do they kill the people who get sent to the crystal?

"None of them are here. At least I've never seen any. They're superior to this place- and to us."

I don't know what to say to that. I don't know what to say about a lot of things in this place, so I bow my head, thinking. We get our food, and I slip on the handcuffs, as repulsed by the feel of the metal as I was yesterday.

"Chloris," I force myself not to think about the cold restraint locked on my wrist. "There has to be at least thirty of us here, and less than a dozen of them," I nod toward the Saguinox. I want to ask why we can't do something to escape, but I remember what happened yesterday and how she ignored me. "Why aren't they afraid of us? Of the others like you?"

"They've locked our powers," she answers sadly.

Powers? I almost fall off my chair. My mind is racing with half finished thoughts, and disorganized ideas, so I take a deep breath before continuing, even though my head is humming with activity. "Does everyone here have powers?"

I attempt to sound casual. We're whispering so low it's difficult to hear, but I don't care because I need answers. Possibilities. Anything.

"Not humans." *Not you.*

I look around. There are only a few non- humans, and they're heavily covered. One looks like Chloris, but she's blue. Another is small and dwarf -like, with earlobes reaching past her shoulders. One more looks human, but I passed by her yesterday and saw hooves where feet are supposed to be.

"Why are they taking so many of us, and so little of

you?" I muse out loud.

"It's harder to catch us," she whispers. "And your blood tastes better. Sweeter."

I stare at her in horror.

"That's what I hear anyway," she finishes quickly, try- ing to assure me she wouldn't know firsthand.

I swallow, my mouth dry as if someone has forced sand down my throat. "What the hell is going on?" I breathe, trying hard to take it all in.

"The same that goes on everywhere," she answers bit- terly. "Power. It's not just a human trait. It's an *every- thing* trait."

"Does all of your kind know about the Saguinox and what they are doing?" I ask.

She shakes her head. "There are things you know nothing about, Kenna. There are whole worlds hidden from you. The Saguinox aren't the only bad guys out there. Ever since the Elemental witches fell, our universe has been in chaos. No one is safe anymore."

"We have to get out," I blurt out the thought before I can stop myself.

She shakes her head, almost angry. "Impossible. *He* will find us."

"Who is this 'he' person everyone is referring to? What does 'he' do that we're all so afraid of?" I snap back.

"He kills."

"We'll die if we stay here anyway!" I almost shriek.

Her eyes widen in fear, and we both glance at the guards still marching around us. One glances our way, and Chloris's throat bobs from her nervous swallowing.

We continue to sip the tasteless liquid for a few moments longer until he passes, the butt of his gun gently nudging my neck.

"He doesn't just *kill* you, Kenna," she hisses. "He digs into your mind, and pulls out your darkest fears, then he makes them come to life. Your heart, your mind, your body, *your soul*, dies. *Every* part of you dies."

I absorb her words, scared, but not so scared I ask, "What's your power?"

"It won't help us anyway. Can't use it." She sounds sad again.

"You're a shape shifter," I say, ignoring her comment. "What do you shift into?"

Her lips are clenched tight. "This and that."

"Chloris! This is important. What do you shift into?"

She shakes her head, stubborn, refusing to tell me.

"Chloris," I growl in warning, forcing her to look at me. "I will scream right now if you don't tell me. You know I will, too," I'm not sure if I would. She doesn't know me enough to call my bluff though. I can see her thinking, and her eyes are blinking rapidly as she decides.

"Fine," she almost snarls. "It won't help us much anyway."

"What do you shift into?" I ask for the third time.

"Plants."

"*What?*" I jerk up.

"Shh! Quiet down!" she cautions in an annoyed voice, bowing her head lower. "I can shift into plants okay?" She glowers at me from the corner of her eye.

"Like flowers and stuff?" I ask in disbelief.

She turns a full glare toward me. "I'm sorry I don't have these cool powers like your dumb spandex wearing superheroes do, but my powers definitely come in handy when the rest of you carnivorous creatures are half starved and dying!"

Her voice ends in a shrill, and the two girls next to us look curious before glancing away. The small movement is enough to set Chloris off, and she's doing something funny with her head. She's glaring and avoiding my gaze at the same time. I can tell she's too mad to talk. I've hit a sore spot somewhere, but for the life of me I can't tell what it is.

The guards make their usual rounds, unlocking the cuffs from our hands. When the bell rings, signaling the end of breakfast, we stand, and begin walking, almost marching to dispose of our silverware.

The early sun is out in full force this morning, and it taunts us with a taste of freedom we can't have. I never considered myself a rebel before, but I'm having a really hard time keeping a low profile. Physically, it's painful, but mentally it's driving me crazy- literally. Involuntarily, my mind searches for the other voice in my head. I feel myself drifting around, but nothing's there. I'm relieved.

I glance at Chloris again, but her eyes are downcast, and she personifies surrender. I don't want to, but a part of me is thinking I need to search for another ally- one who is less content with the state of her incarceration. My eyes move casually around. I don't dare look behind because that would stand out as an anomaly to our perfect lines. It takes a few minutes but I catch a fleeting glimpse of blue skin when a nasty blast of wind pushes the side of her robe back. It's quick, but it's enough, and I make up my mind to zero in on her. She has similar features to Chloris, with the exception of blue skin so dark it could be black. *Please let her shift into something terrifying and poisonous,* I pray silently. Then I sigh because with the way my luck is going, I wouldn't be surprised if she told me she shifts into water.

The labor is as intense as it was yesterday, and though I'm better at feeling for the Braxi, it takes effort to dig, bend, crouch, and repeat. To keep myself sane- as sane as any crazy person can be- I play a game in my head. Any crystals found smaller than the nail on my pinky was worth fifty points, perfect Braxi were worth one hundred, and broken or smaller crystals were negative thirty five. By the time my day was done, I was down to negative eighty five.

My math was fast, but my digging skills were lacking. I did, however, manage to hide another sledgehammer. It was a small victory, but it gave me a moment of happiness that I desperately needed.

Everyday it's the same routine. I wake up in a red filthy dress, and fall asleep dirtier than before. I forget what pants feel like, and I can barely recall the motions of chewing.

Every night I sleep with the depressing knowledge that every moment spent here is a moment living in hell.

CHAPTER 15

I get my chance to form a new alliance the ninth morning. Two more are chosen for the crystal, and those of us who are lucky -if you would call it that- enough to remain a day longer are herded back for breakfast. There have been no new inmates since my arrival, and I'm curious as to why that is. Once the crystal takes all of us, there would be no workers left. Shouldn't they be out scouting for more potential slaves? Maybe their priorities lie elsewhere- like figuring out a way to kill off all the humans. My pessimistic thoughts both depress and anger me.

My line has become two shorter today so I'm moved up away from Chloris and closer to "Mystique" as I've begun calling her in my mind. Her scaly skin reminds me of the azure X-men character. It makes me think of my old life before all of this. Everything here is strange, new, and cruel, and in an odd way, she comforts me.

We sit at the table, and I go through the motions of cuffing myself with the old chains. Mystique is eating next to me. I sneak a glance in her direction. I sip the soup, but I'm too preoccupied on how to approach her that I barely taste it. What do I say? We don't have much time so it has to be something short and small, something to grab her attention and keep it. I frown. I don't want to grab anyone *else's* attention either so it has to be discreet. Maybe if I--

"Pshh."

... accidently spill some soup on her then I could help clean her up. That might--

"Pshh! Hey."

I almost dance with joy when Mystique catches my attention. Almost. I settle for a short glance instead. "Yes?"

"You have soup all over your chin."

I use my palm to wipe it off, but I notice she has a slight smile, and I realize this might be perfect.

"Thanks," I murmur. "Can't catch a boyfriend this way, can I?"

She smirks, pointing to a handsome guard who's in the process of picking his armpit for lice. "Don't think you want to."

I wince. "You're right," I say. "All looks. No brains. I think I'd rather be imprisoned."

She holds back a chuckle, and I'm relieved inside. I feel bad that two had to go to the crystal, but I know it was necessary or else I'd never get next to her.

"I'm Kenna."

"Nymphora," she introduces herself.

"So, if you don't mind me asking, what are you?"

She studies me for a moment before answering. "Shape shifter."

Ka-ching! Score for the invisible human. "It must be nice to have a power," I continue with artificial wistfulness. I straighten my guns and aim for the kill. "To have a chance at getting out."

I let the words linger. I almost expect her to look down in fright at the mere hint of escape the way Chloris usually does, but she doesn't, only staring at me curiously.

"I have as much of a chance at getting out as you do," she begins slowly. "My powers are locked here."

"How do they do that?"

She smiles, and it's deadly. "I'd like to know that myself."

Something dark emanates from her, and for a fraction of a second chills cover my body. I wipe away all doubts, and move forward, refusing to look back. "Have you ever been anywhere else besides our cell, this room, or the cave?" I ask. Something occurs to me. "Are we even on Earth anymore?"

She smirks. "Oh, we're on Earth all right."

"How can you know for sure?"

"Other planets don't look like this and they don't smell like Earth either. Trust me, the aliens haven't taken us anywhere."

"How did they take you?"

She hesitates. "A raid. What about you?"

I'm too embarrassed to tell her what really happened. "Kidnapped," I say instead. It's a half truth.

My heart pounds with what I'm about to ask, but I know the bell will ring soon, and who knows how much time we each had here. She or I could be taken to the crystal tomorrow. Things need to happen and they need to happen *now*.

"Nymphora," I say quietly, "have you ever thought about escaping this place?"

I hold my breath for her answer, ready for anything, even for her to start screaming for the guards.

What I don't expect is for her to look me square in the eye. "Every. Damn. Night."

My sigh of relief is audible, and she's amused. "I wish everyone felt the same way," I mutter before I can stop myself.

"Ah." She grins, and I wonder if she knows Chloris. "Just like humans, we're all different. Some of us are... more *cautious* than others." She smirks. "And then there are some of us who are destined to rule the stars."

"Most of us are too *reckless* to rule anything but our own hands, let alone the stars." Chloris's cold voice surprises me so much I hit her, turning around. She's carrying her bowl with one hand, and I give her a puzzled look.

"Guards are coming," she informs us coolly, nodding in the opposite direction. "You two might want to save your conspiracy talks for another time. Next time I might not be so nice to let you know."

I'm surprised by her behavior, but also a little hurt. Of course, she would warn me, wouldn't she? There's something furious in her eyes, and I'm reminded yet again, how much I don't know about her, Nymphora, and this strange place. Another shiver ripples through my body as I catch Nymphora's gaze on Chloris's retreating back.

I realize I'm playing a deadly game.

CHAPTER 16

I haven't been able to sleep for days so I'm not surprised when, hours after being brought back to my cell I'm still up staring into darkness. Sometimes I'm afraid of the stillness, and when that happens I curl myself into a ball and imagine the person I love most.

For the thousandth time I think about my father, and how abandoned he must be feeling. Is he looking for me? Has he stopped? Is he drinking more to fill the void? I can guess the answer to the last question, and it only fills me with more sadness.

I want to cry, but I don't let myself break down entirely because I'm afraid I won't be able to put myself back together. I allow sniveling sobs to come through, hating how weak I sound, but craving the release desperately. I permit myself to think about the idea I might not make it out of here alive. In the real world I have no one to count on, but unlike the real world, aliens and supernatural creatures that aren't supposed to exist surround me. For the first time I find myself wishing I had stayed invisible and unnoticed. What had made me stand out to Rhys? Why had he taken me?

I'm exhausted, physically and mentally. *What if I stop?* What if I simply let go and surrender? Give myself to whatever they want, even the crystal, and let myself fade the way I already was before all this started?

Surrender can be a form of release, a dark part of me whispers. *If I submit maybe I can see my mom again...*

The floodgates open, and I see her as clearly as if she's across from me. When I close my eyes, she's in my memories, and her laughter trickles, linking one image to the next. I see her face, pinched in worry, waiting anxiously after my first day of school. I smell her skin when she hugs me good night, and I can almost feel her hair brushing against my forehead. I remember holding her hands as we walk through grass, the sun creating drops of light that seem to center around the woman who saved me from death eighteen years ago.

Next Rhys's face drifts into my mind. His glowing eyes are soft, and I remember his arms pressed around my body. I recall his warmth, and the hot tingle of his breath over mine. Instead of anger, I'm feeling bittersweet.

Every emotion crashes together simultaneously, spinning, and boiling out of control. I cry, wailing and sobbing in a way I've never done before.

Kenna.

The sigh is so sweet, and it feels sad, too, and damn it every part of me is cheerless. I scream at the top of my lungs. I do it over and over, and over again, until my throat's as raw as my heart. I close my eyes, and pray for numbness because it might be the only thing keeping me alive.

My outburst over, I take a few shaky breaths and open my eyes. My dad's face flickers into my mind again.

Don't let go.

I won't let go. I can't leave him. I wipe my tears, and trace small circles on the floor to calm my breathing. Then I close my eyes and force things I don't want to think about into my head. Who to trust?

With that thought Rhys flickers into my mind again and I start bristling inside. *He* is the reason for this. *He* carried me to my doom. *He* trapped me in this hellhole! But even as I curse him my heart knows it's a lie. *I'm* the one who followed him. *I'm* the one who begged him to look at me every chance he could. I wanted to be noticed, and he made me feel things I've never felt before. I shake my head mournfully. *I'm* the villain of my own nightmare.

Hey now, cheer up. Look at it this way: you're rocking a fabulous dress everyday.

I shoot up, motionless. Silence.

Seconds tick by. "H-hello?"

Kenna.

My name is a caress. I scream when I feel it, physically jumping back. My heart is pounding so hard I hear it in my throat.

"Who's there?"

Not there. *In* here.

A flash of heat warms my head.

Oh my god, oh my god, oh my god. I'm hyperventilating again, my whole body shaking uncontrollably as I try to take in precious air. His voice is in my head again. Is it real? It can't be.

Kenna. Rhys voice sounds amused. *Breathe, like this.*

I can almost feel him breathing with me, taking slow gulps of air, and exhaling them softly.

I'm shaking my head even as my whole body trembles with shock. How can this be possible? His voice is as clear as my own, louder even. I can feel his presence in my mind, and it's just as I remembered: pulsing, intense, and completely glorious.

Glorious? No one has ever said that about me before. Instead of sounding arrogant, he sounds modest and a little pleased.

I squeak with surprise again. "Stop that!" My voice quivers a little. "Stop doing whatever it is you're doing."

Stop this? *And* this? He's sending me flashes of heat, and they send delicious tingles down my body. Slowly my skin becomes less cold, and I can actually wiggle my toes. I'm wondering how he's doing that, how he can be in my head, controlling my body.

"*What* are you?" It seems to be the theme question of my time here.

Saguinox, he answers as if I should know what that means.

"Do you- are you a mind reader?"

He laughs, and the sound is husky, tickling my senses. *No. I think those died out a while ago.*

"Then how can you do this?" *Is this a dream?*

I feel him shrug, but he doesn't answer.

My mind is racing with possibilities. "Is this... Hell? Have I died and gone to Hell?" My voice is small, and a deep sorrow sprouts inside me.

I almost cry when he doesn't reply immediately.

No, he says, before I can embarrass myself and start bawling. *It's real.* There's a catch to his voice, as if he's thinking about something deep. I suddenly wish I could hear his thoughts too.

"Then everything you told me was a lie," I whisper.

Kenna. His voice is a sigh but he says no more.

"You're not even going to deny it?" I snap, thinking about how he saved me from the fire only to throw me into a hotter one.

I wish there was another way...

"Why are you so hot and cold all the time?" I accuse, thinking back to his warm smiles and cool indifference. Maybe that's how they lure their human prey. Hurt, I fight back the sting of tears. "You saved me so you can kill me?"

Somehow he feels my pain. He knows how deep it goes. He does something in my mind, and for a second it almost feels like he's holding my hand. I clasp my fingers together, but they're cold. Another shift ripples in my head, and there's something pleasant coming over my body, humming as it gently spreads over me.

I buzz with pleasure. I can feel his smile. My aches and pains from the last couple of days are being massaged out, which isn't possible, but the sensations he's creating in my head make everything feel pleasant.

"Why are you doing this?" I stretch to feel more.

I like it when you feel good, he says. Another hot blush instantly fans through my face, and I look away.

He laughs. *You're adorable, Kenna.* Which only makes me feel *less* adorable, and acutely embarrassed. I tell myself he's a cold- blooded human kidnapper, but the warm tingles inside my body make it hard to remember that.

Unexpectedly, I'm bombarded with sights, and feelings, and sounds. At first it's coming so fast I feel like I'm right in the middle of a twister. I see colors, and they're so intense I want to shield my eyes.

Sorry, he apologizes.

The images come again, but this time they're muted so I can see without hurting. He shows me a door opening, then a flash of light. A thunderous roar is heard, and it sounds like waves crashing. He blinks, and I realize what I think are waves are actually a sea of human faces applauding. He's sharing his first memory of landing in Hugo. The adoration from the crowd is so potent he can still feel the vibrations from it weeks later.

Abruptly, I draw back. *Why are you doing this to us when you feel something like that?* I ask bitterly. *They love you, Rhys. And you turn us into slaves.*

It's complicated, Kenna.

No, you're *making it complicated!* I retort back. *Fix it. Help us get out of here.*

He sighs. *You'll survive, Kenna.*

Maybe. I doubt it.

You will, he insists.

"How?" *Will* you *save me?*

Silence.

No. His voice sounds raspy.

Didn't think so. "Then it's going to be pretty damn impossible, isn't it?"

Another silence. *Do you want me to leave?*

No. "Yes."

Kenna. Rhys's voice is a whisper, and it's filled with a hint of longing.

Hot and cold, I think angrily.

When he leaves I cover my face with my hands, knowing I'm truly alone in my prison, and in my head.

CHAPTER 17

The next morning I awake with less soreness in my body, but my mind is completely battered. I have a pounding headache, and my veins are pulsing like they're going to burst.

"All clear."

The doors open, and I step wearily out. The usual Saguinox guard is not here. Instead, the female guard from the cave is standing at the end of the hall, alert. I suck in a breath when I recognize her as the one who almost caught me down at the caves. Her spiky blonde hair looks pointier in the dreary room, and a nose ring glints menacingly underneath the glare of hot lights. Her hair is cropped short to her head, and the chains on her belt and pants make her look sinister. She carries herself like a Goth, but her glowing eyes are amber, and the furthest thing from black.

"All the females will be coming with me," she informs us. Her announcement is met with varying degrees of horror, and she smiles, relishing the fear. "The men will stay behind." She pauses, making certain all attention is on her. "They will wait for the crystal."

Shock ripples through us, and my eyes can't help but go to the two men near me. One is going to vomit, and the other is very thin, and seems to close his eyes in acceptance. The girl across from me is silently sobbing, barely touching the man next to her. His eyes are still closed, and he's breathing heavily. Even though they've probably never talked, both have lived side by side for days, eating, working, and breathing together. That sort of relationship makes a different kind of connection, one that distresses when severed.

The guards gesture to us, and we begin marching. Even though it's forbidden I glance back for one last look. One still has his eyes closed, his face more serene than I've ever seen. The other has his eyes open, and they're following us.

He sees me turning, and stares at me in shock. My gaze doesn't leave his though, and I try to say with my eyes, what I can't with my mouth. He seems to understand, and he gives me the slightest hint of a smile. As I watch, something comes over him. He clenches his jaw, staring at the guard following us. His hands curl into fists at his sides. He's slowly straightening his back, and he winces like it's painful, but he ignores it, arching his back, raising his head, and standing tall.

Defiant.

For one dangerous moment he is as tall as the guards.

That's the last image I see before I force myself to turn away. With one blink he is gone from my vision.

I didn't even know his name, but I play his face in my mind over and over again to make sure I remember what it looks like to stand tall.

* * *

We're moving toward a part of the compound I've never seen before. My heart is pounding with the adrenaline of what I want to do. I sneak secret glances around me, desperate to glean as much information as I can. Dreary gray walls are all I see. We're shuffling our bodies, marching softly, surrounded by four guards who are as mute as we are.

After a couple minutes I notice I'm no longer on concrete. Instead we're walking on wooden floors now. They're shiny and strangely clean. Seconds later we enter through a door. My eyes drift up, and I see a glimpse of white ceilings and a door before I'm ushered through it.

The first thing I feel is warmth. Sweaty air swirls around me, and goose bumps shoot down my body. Then I see the floor, and it's completely white, like thick cream. The white is spotless, and very shiny, and I can't help but wonder how they keep it so clean. Immediately I hear scrubbing sounds, and out of the corner of my eye I catch sight of pale hands scouring the ground. We take a few more steps and stop, one body behind the other, still in two perfect rows. We shift until our shoulders almost touch, facing inward and wait.

The Saguinox female is walking in the center, slowly examining us. When she gets to me, I lower my eyes, holding my breath. The seconds tick by before she finally grunts, moving to the person next to me. Nymphora catches my eyes, mouthing *what is going on?* I only shake my head in answer because, really, I'm the newbie here. *She* probably knows more than me.

After many torturous minutes the Saguinox walks back to the center and claps her hands for our attention. I roll my eyes because it isn't necessary, considering the only sounds heard are her heavy walking. I glance up as she begins to talk, and my eyes widen as I notice something behind her.

A door.

It's barely visible, neatly camouflaged just like the windows and doors on their ships are. My curiosity piqued, it takes every ounce of willpower to look away.

"The one thing you all have in common are the disgusting smells that roll off of you like shit. We have pets on Sangine that smell less than you," she snickers. I grate my teeth in anger. "No one can be offered smelling or looking like you do."

My heart clenches in my chest. *Offered?*

"This is the bathing room." She gestures up and around, but I know better than to raise my head to look. "New offerings will be given to you to wear. Your job is to clean yourselves and make your body presentable. If you're around filth enough, you start to stink like it. And I'm tired of smelling shit."

My chest is squeezing itself, and I glance at Chloris. She looks as sick as I feel. I'd never seen a green face go white before.

The guard's voice is hard as she continues. "Escape is an illusion. Should you attempt, he will find you, and you will be very sorry." With the standard Saguinox warning issued, she turns her back, and walks out. We're left with three smirking guards who suddenly look very interested in us and I want to vomit.

"You may go," she calls to us over her shoulders, but we're not sure what she means or where to go. I look up, and gasp at what I see. My eyes drift over white walls, and white floors. To the side of us are golden curtains. I assume they're shower curtains because there are white tiles underneath. A showerhead peeks through, glinting. To the other side of us is a petite fountain. It's gorgeous and grand, something found in aristocratic homes in ancient Greece. Blue water shimmers inside, and everything is so beautiful I almost forget where I am. This place is a stark contrast to our prison cells. Just being here makes me feel cleaner.

"What. The. Heck." Nymphora whispers to me, sliding closer. "They work us all day, then they want us clean and bring us to a place like *this*?"

I shake my head. "I don't understand. Do you think they're planning to sacrifice all of us in one final, grand offering?"

She looks bleaker than I've ever seen her. "I don't know."

None of us are sure what to do so we follow each other. One enters into a shower stall, and slips her dress off, leaving it hanging on the shower curtain. I glance at the guards, and they're watching us with hot gazes. One

in particular is staring hard at Chloris, his gaze too forceful for my liking. My hands curl into fists, and I resist the
urge to smack the smiles from their faces. I'm stubborn,
and I endure as long as I can. Before long, hot air from
each stall drifts over, beckoning me. I can smell dirt and
sweat on my body, and the warmth is so delightful I finally give in.

Raising the heavy golden curtains, I marvel at the
clean tiles, and the shiny showerhead. It looks more expensive than anything I've ever been able to afford. The
irony doesn't escape me: I'm locked in a prison, worked
to death, but dressed in couture red, showering in a pala-
tial bathroom.

This is so sick.

It reminds me of prisoners on death row. The night before they're sentenced to die they get to choose any meal
they want. It can be as elaborate as they desire, one last
piece of heaven before they're shut out forever. That
thought leaves a dry taste in my mouth, and I don't enjoy
the shower as much as I want to.

Pulling off my dress, I hang it over the shower curtains. It's not very high and my head and neck are still
visible. I turn a knob and instantly hot water cascades
over my skin, making my hair heavy. My brown locks
turn black when wet, and I move it to the side, clutching
the showerhead. I can hear the deep voices of the male
guards, and I give them my back, seething with hatred. I
hear fabric slipping down, and I turn just in time to see
one take my dress, grinning wickedly as his eyes travel
down my skin.

My hands are hot, and I lift my fist, but the sound of something smoldering distracts me. *What the--*

I gasp as I look down, seeing my small fist *smoking* under the water. I shout out, but the water overpowers my cries. I look frantically around to see if anyone notices, but no one does, enjoying their last bit of comfort before the doom. Nymphora is beside me, and she looks curious at my frantic expression. I raise my fist to show her, but the smoke is gone, devoured by a torrent of water. Her expression is puzzled, and I turn back, shaking with a new fear.

Something's wrong with me. Rhys's voice in my head, and the strange hotness in my body. I try to cover every inch of my skin with water, desperate to drown out the heat inside.

Nymphora walks by, wrapped in a red towel. She hands me the one in her hands, and I wrap it securely around my chest before stepping out. The first things I notice are the other girls. Some are taking showers for a second or third time, basking in the little comfort. Others are lounging around, sitting on the ledge of the fountain. They don't talk much because there isn't much to say. For an instant, the sight looks normal like a bunch of girls having a spa day. Nymphora, with her blue skin steps into view, and the picture breaks, replaced with a more stark reality.

The second thing I notice is there are no guards in sight. I stop short, blinking, but no glowing eyes appear. I'm not stupid enough to think of escape, but my mind is anxious as another idea sprouts.

"Nymphora," I talk casually, standing beside her. "Do you see what I'm seeing?"

She glances around nonchalantly, lazily turning her head. "No guards."

"Exactly," I murmur. We both catch each other's eyes, thinking the same thing.

"We probably don't have much time. But it's not likely we'll get another chance."

She's nodding. "Yes. We'll need someone to watch for us, warn us when they come." Simultaneously, we both search for a spot of green. It doesn't take long to find Chloris. She's off to the side, away from the group. Her eyes are half closed, and she looks deep in thought.

"Maybe I should be the one to ask her," I glance at Nymphora. "Something tells me you two aren't the best of friends." Her nostrils flare out in agreement, but she doesn't elaborate further. There isn't a lot of time so I don't hesitate, strolling with determination forward.

"Hi Chloris."

She opens one eye to look at me. "Aren't you supposed to be plotting something stupid and deadly right about now? No one's around to catch you."

It doesn't surprise me she's noticed the absent guards.

"Funny, you should say that," I begin, trying to sound light.

Both her eyes open, and she's staring as if she can read my mind.

"I was hoping that maybe you could do me a favor."

"No."

I swallow because she's definitely mad at me. "Chloris," I try again. "You know as well as I do what this means." I hold my hands out, gesturing to my newly cleaned body. "You heard her. We're *offerings*. We're not meant to ever leave this place." She flinches, and I press harder, coming closer. "There *is* hope. We *can* escape. But we can't do it without your help." I plead. "We're as good as dead here, Chloris. Can't you see that?"

She's looking away from me, staring at the floor.

Precious time slips away with each passing moment.

"Help us," I urge her. "Help yourself. Help this *world*."

I didn't mean to sound as dramatic as I did, yet when the words leave my mouth I know I'm right. "If we stay here, no one will make it out to warn the people. The Saguinox will take us all." I shake my head. "Nothing will ever be the same."

That seems to jolt her a little bit, and she glances up at me. "Nothing will ever be the same for you no matter if I help you or not."

I look away because she's right. Even if I make it out of here, I'll never be able to live the same life, knowing there are creatures like Chloris and the Saguinox out there. My dad's face drifts into my mind, and a fresh pang of homesickness stabs at my heart. "Help me. Just give us a chance."

Her eyes are unblinking. "You don't know what you're getting yourself into with her," she finally says, nodding to Nymphora.

Something cold comes over me with her words. "It doesn't matter. We have to get out of here."

She gives me a look that says *you've been warned.* "I'll help you," she agrees.

I breathe a sigh of relief and I almost hug her. "Thank you."

She doesn't say anything and she doesn't look happy.

"We need you to watch for the guards, and warn us when they come. We're-"

"I don't need to know what stupid thing you're about to do," she interrupts. "You just do what you need to do, and I'll play my part."

"Can you give us a whistle or something if you see them?"

She whistles, and the sound is perfect: low, but high pitched enough it travels. Another whistle answers back, and we turn. Nymphora is giving us the thumbs up. This seems to distress Chloris more, and without a word she walks off, moving slowly to the entrance.

I rush to Nymphora. "Ready?"

She gives me a hard look and says with a smirk, "Of course."

I point to the door on the opposite side of us. It's behind the fountain, and is barely visible inside the wall. I'd only notice it because there was a black line as thick as a piece of hair visible in the light. "It's a door. They're good at disguising entrances."

"Wouldn't doubt it."

"I'm good at not being seen," I inform her, still amazed something I hated my whole life might be the only thing keeping me alive.

She lifts a perfect blue eyebrow. "So am I."

We smile at each other in understanding. "Let's go."

My heart is pounding, and adrenaline is pulsing from my core, but I manage to move with casual nonchalance. It feels like forever, but I'm sure it's only several seconds before we reach the white wall. A few girls are having whispered conversations, yet it's too quiet. My eyes find Chloris to reassure myself she's there, and I spot her almost instantly, leaning against the door, head bowed. She looks so alone. A stab of regret hits my conscience. I look at Nymphora's blazing eyes and I know I've done what is best.

I signal with my hand, and Nymphora moves forward, blocking my small body with her taller one. Fingers fumbling, I try to find something on the wall to hold onto; maybe a latch or handle, anything. I press both my palms on where I think the door might be and push it sideways, like I'm moving a sliding door. A soft click, and I still, sucking in a fast breath. I push again, harder this time, and the door moves.

"I got it," I whisper to Nymphora.

"Go in. Quickly!"

I don't wait to be told twice. I slide the wall, wincing when it makes more noise than I want. When the space is wide enough, I slip my body through.

"Nymphora," I whisper urgently. "Come in."

She does, struggling to fit her tail in, and I slide the door further back. When she's inside, I push it until it's an inch from being closed.

Alarmed, I voice a sudden thought in my head. "What if we can't hear Chloris?" It's too late now, and I want to kick myself for my impulsiveness.

"We will," Nymphora assures me. "She saw you go through. She knows where we are. She'll come here to warn us," she says confidently. I close my eyes in relief. So Chloris *was* looking.

Suddenly, I smell something burning.

The scent is sweet and smoky at the same time, like rotten beef over a frying pan or burning rubber in syrup. The smell is so pungent I taste it in my mouth.

Flesh.

CHAPTER 18

We're in a hallway, and it's elaborately carved with swirling designs inside and on the pale walls. The design's so exquisite I can't help but wonder if corridors in Heaven are like this. When I peer closely I notice stained glass pieces decorating one side of a wall. They're meticulously cut out, each piece a perfect puzzle part to another. The colors are stunning, flashing deep jewel tones that make my senses ravenous for more. I'm so busy looking at each individual part I don't see the whole picture until I move, taking a step backward. What I see makes my skin crawl. I hear a sharp intake of breath and I know Nymphora has seen what I'm looking at.

Eyes. A dozen haunting, glowing eyes peek out from every which way, all looking up at one thing: a crystal. The eyes are staring at it, worshipping the precious stone like a god. Maybe it is. The crystal reminds me of the Washington monument with its elongated sides, and triangular top. It glitters brighter than the eyes, and I'm transfixed by its startling clarity. I lift a finger to touch the glass, and it's hard, cold- unreal.

Nymphora shudders. "Something so beautiful shouldn't be so evil."

I can't tell if she's talking about the crystal or the Saguinox. Maybe both.

The terrible smell continues to assault my senses. I want to gag. "Do you smell that?"

She sniffs the air, her blue nostrils flaring out. Something's burning. She looks at me, and I'm sure we're thinking the same thing.

"I think it's coming from over there." I point to a double door at the end. It's wide and like the one we slid from there are barely any lines to indicate an entrance. Even though I don't want to, my body ambles over, hesitant. Briefly, I wonder if there are cameras, but I doubt it. From what I'm learning about our captors, their arrogance prevents them from thinking anyone can do what we're about to try.

This time there are handles, one on each door. I pull at the golden bars, grunting from the effort. "Locked," I say with aggravation. "Damn it."

I move to the side and let Nymphora try.

She tugs at it, pushing back on one side of the door with one hand, while pulling the side next to it with the other. She struggles, but the double doors remain still. She hisses. "If only my powers worked."

I scan around, searching for anything of use, but the corridor is empty. I look at the stained glass painting. "Hmm."

I walk over, and attempt to take a piece off.

"What are you doing, Kenna?"

I'm too focused on what I want to do to answer. The little pieces are glued tight together so it's hard to tell where one begins and the other ends.

"Kenna?" she prods again.

One hand is flat against the glass, and the other is delicately trying to pry it apart. "I'm trying to get a piece out so we can use the edge to pick the lock."

She makes a sound from behind me. I turn back, letting out a breath.

"It's worth a shot," I say, a bit defensive when I see her incredulous expression.

She shakes her head. "*Not* your best idea."

"Desperate times call for desperate measures. Do *you* have a better idea?"

"Actually." Nymphora glances at the lock underneath the handles again, pensive. She turns back, smiling deviously. "I think I have something that might work." She lifts a finger up, and I watch in utter amazement as one blue fingernail starts to elongate slowly, the tip thin and pointy like a needle.

I take in a sharp breath. "I thought you said your powers are locked."

"They are." She looks at the shiny blue nail. "*This* isn't my power. It's a part of my body."

"You have six inch claws inside your body?" I ask in amazement. "That would've been nice to know before."

She snorts. "What can I do with these? Scratch the Saguinox to death?"

"Maybe."

She rolls her eyes.

I kneel beside her as she gently maneuvers the pointy end of her nail inside the keyhole. I've never picked a lock before, but I don't reveal that. "Just poke around until you hear a click or a gear shift," I advise.

Her eyes narrow in concentration. She jerks back, yelling "Ow!" She pulls her nail out. She looks annoyed, as she picks the broken piece off with her other hand. "It broke."

"It'll grow back, right?" I ask, worried.

"Yeah. By tonight, probably."

"We can't wait that long!" I shriek.

She sends me a cool glance. "Relax. I got nine more." She flashes me her hands. Her pinky is growing, unsheathing like a fragile sword. The end is even smaller and pointier than her index nail had been.

"Oh." I wonder if I look as sheepish as I feel. "This place is making me dumb," I mutter.

She's laughing when she says, "The jury's still out on that one."

I give her a look, but I don't reply. Within moments, this nail breaks too, but I don't freak out because her other pinky expands, elongating until it's touching the door.

"I think I'm pushing too hard," she thinks out loud. I hold my breath in anticipation. *Come on,* I think. *Work!* Then there's a heavy click, followed by a heavier, relieved sigh from me.

She gives me a triumphant smile. "One for us, zero for the glowing aliens."

"Um, I think you mean *five* for the glowing aliens, and one for us," I correct, thinking about the people lost to the crystal.

She shrugs. "If you want to look at the glass half empty..."

"Shh." I hear sounds. Something is sizzling from the inside. I open the door a crack, just enough to see through. A soft breeze hits me and I'm reminded I'm naked beneath my red towel.

The female guard who took us to the bathing room this morning is standing with her hands behind her back, inspecting two figures in red robes. My heart jumps to my throat as I recognize the two men from before. Both are standing with their heads bowed, still as statues. I see a door, half opened from behind them, and I know they've been "cleaned" in preparation for this moment. The robes look fresh and the scarlet color is brilliant against the white walls.

Like the hallway we're in and the bath room, this space is completely white. The room is large, and it isn't an extension of the building. The ceiling is pyramid shaped, and seems to be made from a combination of Styrofoam and plastic, clearly alien made. The top seems to glimmer, sparkling gently. Even the colorless floors have a slight glean to them, reflecting light from its surface.

Crystals and ice.

The room is a paradise of white, and deceptively serene. Looming ahead, and taking up half of the enormous room, is a large crystal. *The* crystal.

It's unlike anything I've ever seen before. From afar I can see the white stone, pulsing, vibrating as loud as an ocean. I'm reminded of Rhys's eyes, because the crystal appears to be colorless, but the opposite is actually true. There are many colors swirling inside, shooting from the base to the top and down again. The crystal is glinting, and shimmering with a radiance that's strangely mesmerizing. As it pulses, the little Braxi crystals jut out, and then back in. *The stone looks like it's moving because the Braxi crystals vibrate,* I realize. Is the crystal made up of millions of Braxi then? I wish I could get closer to find out, but I know it's not a good idea.

A white bowl is on top of an altar a few feet from the base. Two pallid pipes are attached to the stand, and my eyes travel the length of it to the bottom of the crystal. Small nails attach the pipes to the monstrous stone. The pipes aren't human made. Even from afar, I see movement within them. As the crystal pumps, the white pipes reciprocate the vibrations, until the two are moving as one. The dance makes me think of ocean waves rocking back and forth, and I question how they don't crash.

There are no other guards beside the woman, but more aren't necessary. An air of defeat surrounds the two men, and I wonder if they can sense death standing five feet away. The female speaks, but her words can't defeat the roar of the crystal, and the sounds are lost before they ever reach me.

The first one to go is the smaller man. His stooped shoulders, and heavy steps show how sick he is. The guard has no patience for it, and kicks him. He falls to the floor like a broken doll, which makes her angrier. She hits him in the stomach, and I don't have to hear the sounds to know the pain he feels. She drags him back on his feet. He's swaying, rocking because it's painful to stand.

The crystal is getting louder, humming like a slumbering giant. She notices because she glances back. It's shimmering and more colors are visible. Purple, yellow, and oranges coil together, twisting into ropes inside.

His hand is around her shoulders. She helps him walk to the crystal. When he nears it, he begins to fight, trying to shrink back. It's as if he can sense what the crystal wants, and he's using his last few breaths to resist. His attempts look futile, and it isn't long before he's next to the giant stone, violently shaking beside the alien guard.

With terrified anticipation I watch as she slips the robe back from his body, revealing a sliver of pale skin. The ruby cloth hangs on his thin shoulders as a cape. She holds out his hand, pressing it into the wall of the crystal. Instantly, the stone sparkles like it's turned on. A rush of colors shoot up and down, and the man screams. It's a terrifying sound. I flinch.

She takes a step back, yet the man remains immobile, frozen with his feet to the ground, and his hand intimately pressed to the crystal. A flash of metal catches my eye, and she pulls back revealing a small katana sword. Before I can anticipate what she's doing she raises the sword and plunges the sharp tip through the man's hand and into the crystal.

Instantly blood oozes out, as red as the cloth around my body. His screams are never ending, and the crystal absorbs it all. Blood trickles down, but before it can fall, it's sucked into the stone. The millions of Braxi crystals are taking his life force, consuming the most precious parts of him. A faint blush covers the base of the crystal, and as more spurt forth, the pink color travels further up. Each vibration causes the scarlet liquid to move higher, pumping like fish swimming upstream.

Soon the crystal's shrieking becomes louder than the man's. The guard moves behind the man, doing something to him that I can't see. I press my face against the door, peering closer.

She stays behind him for a half minute longer, then steps back, ripping the crimson cloth from his shoulders. His naked body is revealed, bony and abnormally pale. The cloth falls to the floor, light as a feather, burning a picture in my mind's eye.

Suddenly a sharp yell pierces through the roar of the crystal, and my eyes swerve to the second captive. He falls back, a crazed expression on his face. I follow his line of sight and let out a shriek, hitting my face against the door.

"Kenna!"

Nymphora's voice seems far away. All I can see, hear, or feel is the crystal. It's a blaze of even more colors now, pulsing violently against itself. Bile rises in my throat as I finally comprehend what is happening.

He's being sucked into the crystal.

His arms go first. When they touch the crystal, his limbs freeze, motionless against the vacuum absorbing him. After that his chest is next. His skin is pulled, violently suctioned into the interior of the stone like dye dispersing in water. For one terrifying second I see his skin peeled from his body. His face turns away in agony, attempting to escape. But as the Saguinox say, escape is an illusion. The crystal allows him to take one frantic breath, teasing him as it lets go. The second he pulls away the crystal returns full force, sucking him, stripping skin off his face. I see bones and muscles before the guard kicks him from behind, pushing him into the crystal forever.

Loud gurgling sounds emanate from the stone, and the heat travels until even I can feel the hot air as the crystal burns. The smell of smoldering skin wafts through the crack in the door. I hold my breath even as I hear Nymphora making choking sounds.

But the crystal isn't done.

The guard watches his body melt into the stone as a hundred blurry faces rush forward to devour the meat.

"Kenna! Chloris is whistling." Nymphora's pulling me, but I can't move.

My body is frozen.

I watch the pipes pulse in frenzy, and the gurgling sounds get louder. Unexpectedly, something bursts from the bowl. My eyes widen in shock.

"We have to go, Kenna!"

Blood spews forth like a fountain. Within seconds crimson liquid fills the bowl, brilliant against the stark white.

"*Now!*"

All I can think about as Nymphora pulls me away is my first thought about this place had been right.

The color red means death.

CHAPTER 19

We're running, moving as fast as we can. Nymphora pushes the door aside, and Chloris's panicked face greets us.

"Get out!" she hisses. But we're already moving. Nymphora slides through, and I go next, trying to shove the hard door back in place.

"...to line up when you are finished," the guard is speaking, his voice low and deep. My heart is beating with panic because the door is stuck. I'm pushing with all my might, but it isn't moving.

"Kenna!" Nymphora's voice is strained. "Turn around. Bow your head!"

I face the guards, desperately trying to catch her eyes, but she's a deceptive picture of demureness, her gaze trained on her toes. Someone's looking at me, and I have no choice but to drop my head, hands clasped loosely in front of me. We've moved into a crowd of bodies, but luckily no one notices our reappearance. Everyone is too focused on the guards.

The door isn't closed, and though the crack is small, the shadows from the opening would be noticeable next to the white walls. I swallow nervously, trying to hide what I can with my body.

There are three guards. The one in the middle is speaking. He has reddish hair with a strong chin. His eyes don't glow as much as the other two, but the air of authority around him is potent. All three hold clean red dresses in their hands. The one speaking lifts a dress up, offering it to a taker. He's scanning the room, waiting, but no one moves. The women look petrified, and remain frozen.

Taking deep breaths to calm my racing heart, I try to look less winded. When I close my eyes images of what I've just seen bombard my mind, flickering on and off like a switch. So I blink, opening my eyes rapidly, drinking in the sight before me to block the pictures. It's no use though. The scream haunts my mind, and I hear it as a broken song. Resisting the urge to cover my ears, I clutch the towel to my chest, feeling the rapid throbbing of my heart. *Please don't notice us.*

"You." The voice is loud in the silent room. He points to us. I freeze. "In the back. With the green scales. Come here."

Chloris lets out a squeal of terror she can't disguise, and my heart goes from beating like a drum to almost stopping. Everyone's turned to look, and I'm shaking, praying they don't notice the unclosed door behind me.

Chloris' steps are tentative, painfully so. Her dread is so palpable the girls move to the side, creating a wide pathway for her to walk by. Her tail flickers nervously behind her, and we all watch with bated breaths as she stands in front of the guard who called for her. I notice he's the same one who watched her earlier, whose gaze was too intense.

He hands her a dress from his arms. "Go into the stalls and change," he orders. A couple sneers trickle from the two Saguinox behind him, and she shrinks back. He raises an eyebrow, daring her to resist. Silently, she takes the dress, and clutches it to her chest as if it can cover her from their gaze. Her quick steps take her into a stall, and there are fluttering sounds as the towel drops.

He points to another, a strawberry blonde with faint freckles covering her skin. "You. You're next." The girl cowers, bowing her head pitifully. "Come now." The guard's voice is soft, almost patient. He talks to her like she's a wounded animal. Looking at her wide blue eyes, she is. "You won't be harmed."

Yeah right.

Nymphora can barely contain her snort, and her nostrils flare out. We watch carefully, suspicion still rampant. The girl lifts her hands for the dress. Her towel isn't tight, and when her fingers leave her chest, the red cloth nearly drops. Swiftly, the Saguinox guard catches it, moving closer to hide her body with his own muscular one. He says something to her, bending his head until his forehead's almost touching hers. She's looking up at him as if she can't make up her mind. I can't either. What sort of trick is this? I expect him to pull the cloth from her thin body at any moment, but he moves back instead. He gestures, and the girl goes into a stall, quiet as a mouse.

No one is sure what to make of what we just saw. The tension lessens since we know we won't be harmed, and each girl takes the offering without a sound. The guards point at women, commanding them over like they're ordering dinner. I'm repulsed, but also relieved. The commotion is enough to cover what I want to do, and turning back, I attempt to push the door back in.

"Nymphora," I whisper loudly for her attention. "The door's stuck. Hurry!" She gives me a startled look, swishing her tail.

"You've got to be kidding!"

I grunt, pushing. "Not. Kidding. Help. Me!"

She makes an aggravated sound, and together we pull and push, heaving with our efforts. The women are slowly disappearing into stalls, and I know it's only a matter of time before we're noticed.

"It's broken," I finally tell Nymphora, halting her movements.

"No, it's not. We just used it!"

"Stop." I grab her arm anxiously. "Look, we're wasting time. We just have to make sure they don't notice."

"And how are we going to do that?" she asks angrily.

I take a deep breath because I don't like what I'm about to say. "By creating a distraction."

Her eyes open wide like I'm out of my mind. "That's going to get us killed faster than you can say the word!"

I take another deep breath, hating my next thought. "Not if it's a distraction they like."

"What does *that* mean?"

I nod to the two guards who are too busy gawking to notice our stares. "Look at how they look at us. The dresses make us beautiful- desirable."

She raises an eyebrow then gestures to the red towel clashing horribly with her blue skin.

"It does," I insist, remembering Rhys's sharp intake of breath when the dress was put on me.

"Personally, I think it makes them want to eat us," she interjects.

I shake my head, ignoring her. "We can, oh, I don't know," I murmur, thinking out loud, "maybe *flirt* with them?"

Her mouth drops open for a solid five seconds. After that moment of astonishment passes, she laughs.

I ignore her outburst, and struggle on. "You, me and Chloris," I say, valiantly trying to speak over her snorts.

Nymphora looks at Chloris, who is incredibly timid leaving the shower stall. She plucks at the dress, lifting it like she wants to hide inside. Nymphora looks back at me, and laughs harder. "Forget it. *That's* not going to happen."

"Fine," I snap, irritated. "*I'll* do it."

She's looking at me, amused, which only annoys me more. I straighten, determined to prove her wrong like our lives depend on it, which they do.

Everything I've ever seen Bree and other popular girls at our school do flitters through my mind. Images of girls lowering their lashes in playful shyness, and lightly touching in flirtatious gestures tumble in my mind, rolling into each other like sand. They always made it look smooth, easy even. I attempt to move with more grace, swaying my hips slightly like I had seen women do in movies.

I glance up, but no one other than Nymphora watches me. She's giving me an I-told-you-so look, and I clench my teeth. *I need to be noticed* now, *more than ever.* Boldly, I walk straight to the red haired guard, whom I'm almost positive is the one in command.

"Excuse me." I attempt to make my voice thick and husky. I point to a scarlet dress. "May I have one," I gulp, "H-honey?"

He's looking at me in utter shock, and for a moment I feel like his mouth is going to stay open from pure astonishment. His cheeks flush, and he bites his lower lip. Something in his eyes glint, and he blinks, hiding it before I can understand it.

"Yes," he says, swallowing hard. He looks a little embarrassed. He's taken off guard, and it's making him speechless. For some reason that knowledge makes me more confident.

I edge closer. Ancient womanly instinct kicks in, and I lock my eyes with his. I have no idea what I'm doing, and the whole time I'm acting this out, another part of me is cringing, wanting to hide under a rock. But I don't back down. I keep my gaze level with his.

I stand tall.

He catches his breath, staring at me, and for the second time in my life I wonder what a man sees when he looks at me.

"Here," he finally says. He hands me the cloth, careful not to touch my fingers. I'm clutching the towel to my chest, and I see his eyes glance there quickly, before he looks into mine.

"Go change."

I hold the dress limply in my arms.

Swiftly, he gives me his back. "Boys," he calls out, his deep voice rumbling in the quiet room. The other two guards look up. One looks slightly annoyed at being interrupted. When he has their attention, he says, "You two go ahead. I've got it here."

"You sure? I don't mind staying longer," the one who looks the most annoyed offers. His eyes never stop moving, staring at us in a way that unnerves me.

"Yes," the red haired guard replies, his voice hard. I see his shoulders stiffen ahead of me. "Go." The command is harsh. "Now!" The two walk off, sending irritated glances back, but they don't argue.

He doesn't look back to acknowledge me as he walks to the entrance. Even though I'm left standing alone, I don't feel rejected. I can't describe the feeling coursing through my blood, but it's something powerful. I glance at Nymphora, who's looking at me with a slightly awed expression.

I hide a secret smile.

It's quiet for the rest of the time we're there; but this time the quiet isn't one filled with fear. At one point, it even feels calm. I keep my eyes trained on the Saguinox guard as I disrobe, but he never turns back to stare at us. Not even once.

I think about what Nymphora said about how like humans, shape shifters are all different, and I begin to wonder if the same can be said about the Saguinox. Rhys's golden eyes flash in my mind. A flutter runs through me.

Without thinking my mind calls out, *Rhys?*

As soon as I say his name, I want to take it back. I don't know what he can do in my head, and I'm scared he might see what Nymphora and I did. I wait with rising panic, but I don't feel his presence in my mind. A minute passes by, and still, I don't sense anything. Strangely, I'm relieved and disappointed at the same time.

I'm one of the last to enter the lines. I walk behind Nymphora like I've done since yesterday. Looking at the floor, I notice faint swirling designs. It's obvious that this place was built with care, yet one hundred feet over these halls is a gloomy and rundown prison. I mentally shake my head again at the paradox of our situation. *It must have something to do with the Saguinox culture,* I think. Cleanliness and beauty before an ultimate gruesome death, I conclude. A chill washes over me that has nothing to do with the thin shift I'm wearing.

Abruptly, I feel hot hands grabbing mine. Chloris grips my fingers, squeezing them before letting go. I gaze at her with surprise. She's breaking an unspoken rule: never leave your spot in line. She pulls the girl in back of her to the front, and she's so surprised she doesn't resist. Then Chloris is beside me, breathless and nervous.

Her eyes are wide, and tremulous when she says, "We're getting out of here *tonight.*"

Chapter 20

I'm dreaming.

I know I am because I'm wearing pants. They're soft and silky, and not the least bit red. Tumbling birds decorate it, and I'm reminded of home. A warm bed. A fast meal. Dad.

I'm on a beach. And even in my dreams I'm a bit embarrassed to be walking in my pajamas on a beach. The waves are soft and gentle, only loud enough to make me feel less alone. Oddly, I'm not cold even though my spaghetti strap tank top is too thin for this weather.

At first it looks a little gray like my mood. The clouds are dim, and leaves from nearby trees look dark, like they've been rained on. The feeling of a calm before the storm comes over me, and I shudder, not liking the serenity anymore.

I stop to sit on a small sand dune that appears beside me. It's as if the sand anticipates what I want and supplies it before I can even ask. When my body touches the grains, they slide over me, lightly covering my body like a blanket. I sigh. I can get used to this, *I think with a wide smile.*

Leaning back, I rest my head on perfect grains of sand. Un-expectedly, the sun peeks through the clouds, valiantly pushing through, until a golden beam swathes me with a circle of warmth. I feel so good my toes curl inward, digging in as deep as they can. I watch the waves play with each other, and my giggle rings out when I notice the color: clear. Completely, and brilliantly clear.

Standing, I brush soft pebbles from my body before running to touch the ocean. It licks at me, teasing me with just the right touch of cool. I make a cup with my hands, then pause as a thought unfurls inside my head. Is this safe to drink? *Impulsively, I take a sip, and I'm glad I do because it's as cool and refreshing as it looks, not salty at all. I wasn't thirsty before, but I'm ravenous now. I lap at the water like I'm a puppy, and the picture in my mind is so ridiculous that I laugh and laugh until my insides hurt.*

"This is a silly dream," I whisper to myself.

I hear my mom's voice in my head. "Silly dreams are the best."

Her voice echoes from my memories, and the usual pang of hurt grips my heart. I let my body drift into the ocean, walking further in.

Amazed, I take in the sight greedily. The water is so clear it's invisible, and I can see through it to the ocean floor. It's white, completely pristine, and devoid of any filth. A killer whale swims by, his dorsal fin two feet above the surface. He circles me, swimming lazily around. I should be scared, but I'm not. He's a gentle giant, and I beckon him closer. When he comes he nudges my feet. I touch his wet skin, marveling at how firm it is. Crouching lower, I peer through the invisible surface as his wide face continues to nuzzle my ankle. Then he makes a little sound and moves away, lazily circling me again. I watch him for many minutes.

Suddenly I feel a tingling sensation down the back of my neck.

"Of all the dreams of all the creatures in all the galaxy, you had to walk into mine."

My heart leaps with excitement. I shouldn't feel happy, but I can't stop the eager breath escaping my lips. When I turn he's watching me, and there's a relaxed smile on his face I've never seen before. I wonder if I have the same smile on my face because he's looking at me as intently as I am looking at him.

"Is this your dream?" I ask, unable to mask my happiness.

He looks adorable when he glances at me. He points to the whale swimming further from us. "Yes, but its turned into a joint effort."

I'm not sure what he means by that, but I don't care. I open my arms wide because I want to hold the ocean, the sand, and the whole world in my lap. I close my eyes and say, "I think we did a pretty good job then."

He moves until he's behind me. "I think so, too."

His breath is near my neck, and I turn around. Instantly, I'm greeted by Rhys's broad chest. In that second I realize he's not wearing what he usually has on. Instead, a white buttoned up shirt is covering his tan body. He leaves a few buttons casually open, and I see a slice of golden skin. Dark shorts go past his knees, and his feet are bare. He looks casual, and very sexy. He can hear my thoughts, and his grin broadens.

I'm too happy to be embarrassed. That's another reason I know this is a dream. I point to my Angry Bird pajamas. "I seemed to have missed the memo about the dress code."

"No worries," he says, flashing another white grin. His smiles are making me delirious, and everything seems to glow brighter and become fuzzier at the same time. I hear soft rustling, and cool air brushes my body before something gentle touches my skin. Looking down I see a long flowing dress. It's red, and the wind picks up the tail of the dress, blowing it and my hair behind me.

"You're so beautiful," Rhys says, his voice thick with everything he feels. His gaze is so tender that I'm hypnotized by it. I feel so happy my heart wants to burst with joy. The red cloth is blowing all around me, and even though he's looking at me like I'm the most exquisite woman on earth, my lungs are having trouble breathing.

"Rhys," I choke out. "Not red. Please, not red."

A look of concern and a flash of guilt cross his face and he says, "I understand." He holds out his hands to me.

"Think of a beautiful color," he whispers to me.

I let him take my hand, and when our palms touch the breeze picks up. A quiet rustling sound is heard, but our eyes never leave each other. His other hand circles my waist. He shoots me another devastating smile, his black hair perfect in the light. He looks down at what I'm wearing.

"Gold?"

"Golden eyes." He looks so sweetly at me I wrap my arms around his neck. I fit his body perfectly, and my gold dress is shining, shimmering as bright as his eyes. We're swaying in the breeze, dancing as the waves play around us. Questions swim in my head, and I know it's important I find the answers, but I bat them away like flies. For once I'm not thinking about escape and staying alive. I am happy, carefree and filled with joy.

"I used to come here when I was a little kid," he tells me. I watch his mouth move, and I continue to even when he catches me. He looks amused.

Dreams are a safe place for doing anything I want.

"Armin and I would sneak off when we could. We didn't do much, just laid around, sleeping. But this place holds some of my best memories."

"I can see why," I say, pointing to the sand. "We need something like that on Earth. It's like they're alive. They moved over me like ants!"

"The particles have a magnetic pull to blood."

I laugh. "That makes absolutely no sense! Blood doesn't contain magnetic properties," I inform him. "Even I know that and I'm a C average in science."

"Now that makes no sense." It's his turn to point out. "You get graded with letters. How do you know how to improve? The letters tell you nothing," he dismisses in his sexy accent.

"How do they grade you in Sangine?" I ask.

His grip tightens on me. "You probably wouldn't like it," is all he says. His lips thin and I know we're talking too much about reality, so I lay my head on his shoulders, listening to his gentle heartbeat.

"You're really very handsome," I finally whisper to his chest.

"And you're really very beautiful," he whispers to my hair.

"Is that why you took me?" The question slips before I can halt it.

Hot and cold. *Right now he's all hot. I don't want him to turn cold. He's already sighing when I say,* "Don't answer that."

"No," he says quietly near my ear. "That's not why I took you. I had no choice, Kenna. I'm wasn't born with freedom the way you were." His voice is filled with such sadness and longing I shut my eyes.

"Let's not talk about this anymore," I whisper.

We move together in a circle, swaying with the water. Slowly doubt creeps into my thoughts: about who he is, what he's done, and why he's sentenced me to die. I hum loudly to cover the noise in my head, and he seems to sense my distress. He hugs me tighter into his chest, breathing in my scent like a starving man.

"I'll make everything better." It's a lie. He can't. I know he can't. He knows it, too. But I nod anyway.

Soon, much too soon, I notice the sunshine waning and growing dimmer. I force myself to step back from him. I gaze into his eyes, trying to memorize the myriad of colors shimmering inside.

"Rhys," I breathe. I don't know what to say, or how to express what I feel. That one word seems to be enough though because he smiles.

"Kenna, you're stronger than you think you are." He holds my face in his hands. "You're special. You're a survivor." He looks deep into my eyes. "Even when everything burns you won't."

Goosebumps rise across my skin. I shiver from his words.

"When I wake up am I going to forget all this?" I suddenly ask him, desperate to know.

He gives me a sexy smile. "No."

Relieved, I grin back, unable to resist him. "So none of this is real?"

"Nope." He's laughing at me.

I pull his face closer to mine. "So none of this is real, and when I wake up I'll remember everything," I repeat softly, my mouth a breath away from his. Suddenly, he's looking at me with intensity and hunger. I think about where we're at and I know it isn't really paradise. I feel his arms around me, and his clean masculine scent drifts through my nose and into my heart. This is paradise. I lean over, and touch my lips with his.

We meet in the middle. As far as first kisses go this is the best one I've ever had. He's soft and hard at the same time. His lips taste as fresh and crisp as the water pooling around us.

When I finally pull back, we stare at each other, breathless. "So when do we get to do that again?" I ask, again, unable to stop myself. He laughs, noticing what a truly impulsive person I am.

All he says is, "In your dreams."

I attempt to frown at him, but a smile is touching my lips.

Then the sky breaks open with a roar, scaring me. It sounds like thunder when the clouds part. The waves greet this noise with their own loud applause, smashing into each other like giants. I can't hear my own thoughts. I clutch him tighter.

He gives me the saddest look I've ever seen, before he's gone, vanished from my dreams.

Chapter 21

SAGUINOX ENCAMPMENT

He wished she hated him.

It'd be so much easier if she could.

Most people would hate someone who imprisons them, and leaves them at the mercy of an alien race. Deep in his heart, he always knew she wouldn't.

He pulls the crystal shard from his skin, winching when blood rushes out. Carelessly, he flips the white stone onto a table. It makes a loud clinking sound as it lands. If Malachi ever saw him do that, Malachi would probably stab him with it. Malachi "honored" him with a piece of the precious crystal many years ago. Its powers allow them to communicate with each other in their minds. It's especially useful during battles, and it's most certainly meant to be taken care of, not thrown carelessly about.

It's also not meant to be used with the enemy. A picture of Kenna flickers in his mind, and his chest tightens. The consequences be damned. It was all worth it.

The pain's more excruciating than usual this time, and he grips his arm, trying to numb the sensations. Somehow, that only makes it worse and he falls back on the bed, shutting his eyes. Even with them closed, he can still visualize the scabs and wound marks littering both his arms. The crystal is a vault of energy, and with the right magic it can be used for many things.

But, like everything, its energy comes at a price.

The marks on his arms won't heal for a while. And even when they do, there will always be reminders on his skin, and especially on his soul.

There's a light knock on the door, and he knows who it is even before it opens. He lets her knock until she's finished.

"Yes, Lenora?"

Her big eyes peek over the door. "How'd you know it was me?"

He sighs. "Most people don't knock on a door to the rhythm of 'Mary had a little lamb'."

She beams. "It's the first song I learned in English!" She closes the door behind her. The other Saguinox think they're mating, and he knows it hurts her when the other warriors stare at her with a smirk. She accepts this, though. It's safer if they think she belongs to him.

He sees her eyes go to the bloody gash on his arm. She bites her lips in worry. "Maybe you shouldn't communicate with her so much, Rhys," she advises softly. "The crystal's going to kill you."

He can't tell her he doesn't really have a choice. Kenna calls to him. "I'm fine," he answers, sounding more tired than he wants to.

He doesn't want to admit it, but Lenora's right. He shouldn't be communicating with Kenna. She'd said he was "hot and cold". She was right. Everytime he felt a pull pushing them closer, reality would seep in, and he'd be reminded of what he was, what he'd done, and what he needed to do still. He should've never gotten close. He didn't have to talk to Kenna to kidnap her. That hadn't been the plan. It had always been Lenora who was sup- posed to get close; Lenora who had such a fascination with all things human. Somehow he'd ended up with a locker near hers, and the rest as they say, is history.

Rhys's eyes are closed, but he knows Lenora's looking at him. She has a soft heart, and is the biggest humanist he's ever met. She loves everything about humans. She would even risk her life for what she believes in. That's why she's one of the few he trusts.

"Maybe we shouldn't have left her in there," Lenora be- gins again, worried.

"It's the only way to keep her safe. You know what's happening right now."

"Maybe if we just told her--"

"No. I already told you what the King plans to do. She won't be able to escape Armin again. You know I had to poison his powers to make him weaker. The King is sus- picious and will have Touchers on us next time." Realizing how he sounds, he softens his tone. "She won't escape again. Armin's too powerful, and now he feels like he's got something to prove."

There's a long moment of silence. "It's just ironic that to protect her we have to put her right in the center of it all."

"It's been done before," he answers, gritting his teeth. The cut from the crystal is burning and aching at the same time. "They won't think to look for her there."

"Were you able to talk to them?" she asks. She doesn't say their name. She doesn't need to.

"Yes. I've leaked the codes and a blueprint of the building to them. They've already sent someone in. He's in the compound as we speak."

"I wish we could go get her. She probably hates us," Lenora says, almost tearfully.

"Not quite."

"Maybe not *you*," she accuses. "But definitely me."

"Lenora," he comforts her for the thousandth time. "One person not liking you in the grand scheme of things isn't so bad."

"I know, but I really liked her. I really like them *all*. I wish... I wish I hadn't been born Saguinox," she confesses softly. "I hate the violence, the way we kill people. The way we conquer."

His whole body tightens with her words. Images of what he's done enter his head like angry bees. Pictures of death flash like a never-ending story.

One in particular stands out.

A battlefield. A girl, starved and dying. He'd been the one to find her. The King had deemed her death as his prize. Young and foolish, he did what he was told. He destroyed her with his hands until her body was unrecognizable. Until her body was as flat as the field they stood on, covered with human debris and dirt.

He pushes the memory out of his mind, clenching his teeth to do it.

"It's all the people know," he answers softly. "It's what we've done for thousands of years."

It's what he's done for a century which is why he, more than anyone, knows what they're risking if Malachi found out what he and Lenora were really doing. He's delivered revenge in the name of the King many times. It always ends with death.

But that's the easy part.

It's what happens *before* death that scares people. Torture. Pain. Annihilation of everyone you love.

He risks it all. Even now, he refuses to think about failure. Too much is at stake. Earth. The universe.

Life.

"It's hard to change something when you've never seen anything different."

"*We* are. *We're* changing it, Rhys," Lenora points out softly.

He allows a trace of a smile to touch his lips. "Yes."

"Truitt will arrive tomorrow. He's been able to round up more men," she informs excitedly.

He's alarmed. Damn Truitt and his hot- headed ways. Did he want them all to get killed? "How does he know we can trust these men?"

"They've all been wronged by the King. They want their revenge."

He shakes his head. "This isn't about revenge. It's about what's right and wrong."

"I know."

He's sure she *does* know. He's just not sure about the rest.

"Truitt says they can be trusted."

He doesn't look at Lenora. "Trust is a fickle thing."

Lenora bites her lips.

He sighs, standing up. He gives her his back, rubbing his temples. He isn't ready for this. Even after a hundred years he's still not ready for this. Dethrone the King? There was a time when he couldn't have even imagined it, and now it's in every move they plan and every word they speak.

Treason.

"There's so much at stake," he says, "Truitt can't just--"

A loud knock interrupts them. They're motionless.

"Sir. The orders have changed." The voice is muffled, but he can hear the urgency in it. "We leave tonight."

Lenora stiffens. "No," she whispers, shocked.

His heart starts to race, accelerating with each passing second.

"Sir?"

"Yes," he calls out harshly. "Get my uniform ready."

Lenora's eyes are wide. "You aren't thinking of really--"

"I need to buy us more time," he interrupts. "They can't suspect me. We need more time."

His hands clench at his sides, trying to control the tension and anger coursing through his body. Kenna's face tumbles into his mind, followed by every creature that's ever come before him. Their lives depended on him.

Everything depends on him.

Suddenly, he can't take it anymore. He turns around swinging, and punches the wall. He doesn't stop when he goes through the plaster and into the metal beams. His fists leaves a dent. The pain isn't enough, but the sounds are loud enough to drown out his pounding heart. There's silence when he's done.

Looking at his raw hands, he's shocked. *A warrior is never driven by his emotions.* Malachi's words drift into his mind, a chant from his childhood.

"I'm sorry."

"Don't be." Her voice is soft. "I've seen worse."

Silence.

"I told myself I'd never be like my father," he confesses quietly.

"You're not."

He thinks about every evil thing he's done. *I'm not so sure.*

When he doesn't respond, Lenora says, "I will pray."

A muscle ticks in his jaw. "It's too late for that."

The war is beginning.

CHAPTER 22

The door slams, jolting me awake. I jerk, and my head hits the cement wall behind me. "Ow!"

My eyes are groggy, and I blink a few times before I can see the shadow standing in front of me. Instantly, I know he's a guard. His eyes glow fiercely in the dim light. I shrink back, using my dress to cover as much of my body as I can. He stares at me for a moment, and I can't see what he's thinking. Inside my chest, my heart is hammering with fear. Swiftly, he closes the door behind him, and when I hear a soft *click* I let out a shriek.

Immediately, I'm reminded of the men from today who had looked at us with too much desire. I don't attempt to find anything to fight with because there's nothing in my cell. Curling my fists, I stand on shaky legs.

"You'll have to kill me first."

He's still hidden in the shadows, but I think I hear a sound from him.

"Do you hear me? You'll never touch me alive!"

He's moving faster than I've ever seen. His body pushes me hard into the wall, and a large hand silences the scream ripping from my throat.

This close I can see his face. He's the one from before, the one who gave me my dress. The one who guarded us from the entrance. I still don't trust him, and neither does my body. My heart continues to accelerate, pounding against my skin.

"Shh," he says, his voice low and strained. "Chloris sent me."

I shake my head. I don't believe him.

"You're lying," I spit out when his hand leaves my face. "Liar!"

Immediately, his hand covers me again, pressing my body firmly against the wall. Barely able to breathe against his palm, I continue to struggle.

"Stop," he hisses. "We don't want them to hear us!"

I'm not sure why, but those words make me stop. I still, letting him cover my mouth.

"Promise me you won't scream."

I hesitate, but see the worried look on his face, and nod in agreement. Slowly, he removes his hand from my face, staring like he expects me to go back on my word at any moment. I keep my promise though, and don't make a sound, even when I see the glint of a knife in his pants pocket.

Tentatively, he backs away, looking at me wearily. "You're quite a handful for a human," he finally says.

I don't reply.

"I'm Kaiden." He pauses as if expecting my name. When it doesn't come, he grins. I'm so taken aback to see a Saguinox smile that I bump my head against the wall behind me.

"Ow!" I cry for the second time in two minutes.

"You're kind of a klutz, you know."

"No, I'm not," I rub my sore spot. "Tonight's just been a rough night." I'm frowning at myself, wondering why I told him that.

He looks empathetic. "Nightmare?"

Unexpectedly, images from my dream flitter to the surface of my mind, and I suck in a painful breath. Quickly, I push them back, burying them with endless magnetic sand.

"In this place? More like a bad *life*," I answer with as much contempt as I dare.

He doesn't seem to take offense, and even agrees. "I bet."

Unable to stop myself, I stare at Kaiden, trying to figure him out.

"What?" he says, when I don't look away. "Do I have something in my teeth?"

"No, it's something worse. You're starting to sound like you have something here." I touch my chest, where my heart rate has returned to normal.

He looks confused for a second before he starts laughing. It feels genuine and oddly out of place in this dark prison. "What's your name?"

"You'll have to earn it first," I answer stubbornly, not wanting to tell him anything about myself.

"Okay."

He doesn't try to press me for more, and we grow quiet, letting the stillness envelope us. He gets up to look around, examining cracks on the walls. He taps it with his fists.

"Pure concrete." He doesn't wait for me to reply before he's investigating the ceiling. His head's almost touching it and he lays his hands flat against the hard surface. He walks the tiny perimeter of the cell, appearing to be searching for something.

"What are you doing?" I finally ask, a little impatient with his presence in my room.

He looks up from where he's bending, crouched near a corner. His answer surprises me. "Damn. This place really sucks."

"No." I gasp sarcastically. "What gave it away? The insane mortality rate?" Instantly, I bite my tongue, wanting to take the words back.

He doesn't seem to mind my seething retort though, and only smiles pleasantly as if we're having a lovely conversation about weather. I can't help but look at him like he's crazy, but he remains indifferent, holding a casual smile that exasperates me.

He leans against the wall with one shoulder, arms crossed, standing confidently and studying me. His gaze is unnerving, and I can't hold it for long.

I'm the first to drop my eyes, studying the worn leather of his boots. The silence stretches into tension-for me anyway. His body's relaxed. That's so rare in this stress filled place I instantly become more suspicious.

"If you're not here to hurt me, then what are you here for?" I ask grudgingly.

"I told you. Chloris sent me."

"Look Kaiden," I try to ignore the way he smiles when I say his name "if you really know Chloris, then you would know she'd never do anything like that. She doesn't trust your kind." A hazy picture of Rhys appears in my head. I push it away. "And neither do I."

"Good." He's rubbing his eyes with his hand.

"What?" I gape at him. "Haven't you heard a single word I've been saying? *I don't trust you!* Now, I don't know what kind of sick game you're trying to play, but-" Unexpectedly, I stop short, my gasp halting anymore words.

He's trying to take out his eyes.

Before I can scream I hear a loud sound.

Kaiden freezes for a fraction of a second before pushing me to the wall and simultaneously covering my mouth. *A growing habit of his,* I think with rising hysteria.

"Shh. Did you hear that?" He's straining, concentrating, but all I hear is the accelerated pounding of my own heart. "Quiet."

We're both silent for so long I'm having trouble standing with the way his body is crushed against mine. Then, before I can say anything I hear it.

Footsteps. Light. Hurried.

I tense, and we stand absolutely still. The footsteps stop right behind my door. Kaiden curses, turning his back to me. I hear his dagger against his jean pockets be-

190 · MARI ARDEN

fore I see it, shining valiantly against the dark. He flips the blade into his other hand. It's obvious he's an expert with this weapon.

When the door opens, I expect to see a trio of guards charging at us with swords raised. What I *don't* expect to see is a slender blue head, peering next to the door.

"Ready?" she whispers.

"*Nymphora?* What... how are you here?" I whisper, completely shocked.

"Chloris drugged the guard."

"*Chloris?*"

"Mouth to mouth poison." Nymphora kisses the air dramatically to show me. "Works every time."

"Huh, so that's why it took so long." Kaiden's defensive stance softens, shoulders sagging, as he moves away from me. Sliding the blade back into his pocket, he asks, "Aren't her powers locked?"

Nymphora shrugs, her slim shoulders rolling gently. "It's that time of the month for her. You know how it gets. Her body starts secreting-"

"Ugh," Kaiden holds up a hand. "No more details, please." He pushes my dazed body ahead. "Let's get the hell out of here. This place is depressing."

I'm shell shocked, and momentarily speechless so I don't argue as we leave, swiftly making our way through the corridor. All the other cells are locked with sound proof walls so I can't hear a thing. We find Chloris waiting anxiously for us at the end. She's standing next to a slumped guard, who is half sitting half lying down. His eyes are still open, but the glow inside them has disappeared. His skin is ashen, and the only alive looking thing about him is his red and wet lips. Chloris's own mouth is scarlet. Her lips look larger than normal, plump as if they've been injected with something.

Nymphora catches me staring at her new look. "Angelina Jolie lips. The only thing about plant shifters I envy."

Chloris frowns at Nymphora, and touches her curvaceous lips, cringing a little. "Forgot how painful that can be," she confesses with a wince, nodding to the dead guard. "It also took longer than I thought. I had to have been kissing him for ten minutes! I need to get these things sanitized when we get home." She points to her mouth, talking about it as if it's not a part of her.

"How is that possible?" I ask. "Once a month your mouth just... plumps up?"

"That's one thing that happens, yeah," she confirms. The look on her face tells me there's more, and it isn't very good.

Nymphora shakes her head. "It doesn't matter if you're human, or shape shifter, women always get the bad end of the bargain."

Kaiden walks by, rubbing his eyes furiously. His fingers touch his eyes again, and he's squeezing like he's trying to pull something out. He makes a sound, then suddenly he's yelling, shouting with pain.

"What the-?" Nymphora runs to him.

"Kaiden!" Chloris sounds worried.

"Shh!" I hiss. "You'll alert the rest of the guards!"

Chloris hurries over, trying to move his hands from his eyes. "What's wrong?" His shoulders shake in violent pain.

"Holy crap, Kaiden!" begins Nymphora.

Kaiden turns and he's laughing, his shoulders convulsing with mirth. Chloris's small hands punch him playfully on the shoulder. "I've forgotten how much of a goofball you are. Need I remind you that we are right in the middle of a dangerous escape?"

Filled with amusement, he answers, "That's the best time for jokes! Makes our deaths seem less imminent."

Gaping, I turn to Chloris and Nymphora, bewildered. "Where did you find this guy?"

"I'm the best at what I do," Kaiden answers grinning. Using both hands, he sticks two fingers into his eyes, pulling out a contact. A glowing half sphere slips from one eye. It falls into his palm like an ember, shining just brightly enough to catch our eyes.

"What is that?" I ask.

"Fake Saguinox eyes," he says. "This is the first one from the lab. They decided I'd be the lucky guinea pig who'd get to try it first." He opens his palms so I can see. It's pretty, in a haunting way. He moves it around his palm, and the colors shimmer like a prism.

"So you put on some fake contacts and that's it? They just welcome you like family?" I ask, incredulous.

"Not quite as easy as that," he laughs.

Nymphora chimes in." Some might consider Saguinox guards handsome, but they got rocks where their brains should be." She turns her gaze to Kaiden. "We're really lucky the warriors aren't here because they wouldn't fall for a trick like *that*." She points to the contact in his hand.

He fumbles with his other eye for a few more seconds before the contact pops out, glowing like a lightening bug. He sighs with relief, and slips the delicate material into a small canister. When he looks up again the first thing I notice are two perfect, *very human* blue eyes.

"Back to business. The guards will change in about thirty minutes. No cameras anywhere except on the exits," he informs us.

Is he human?

"Somehow Cuinn got a hold of their security codes. He gave me some numbers that should override their system for awhile. We're not sure how long it's going to last though so we need to move *fast*." By the time he gets out the last word, we're already moving.

I'm trying to run and think at the same time, but everything is coming together so rapidly I'm actually dizzy. Chloris is beside me, and I clutch her arm, pausing to regain my breath, my balance, and my *head*.

"You okay?" she asks softly, stopping to wait for me. Her voice is huskier, and my eyes travel to her lips, wondering if it's to blame.

"Yes. Chloris, this is crazy. Are we really escaping?"

"Yes," she replies firmly. "We are." She takes my arm, and pushes me along. Never in a million years did I ever think Chloris would be the aggressor in our escape, but her firm hands guiding me forward is unmistakable.

When I look at her, a hundred questions fly through my mind, but deep down the question burning the brightest inside is how can I move on from the memories of this desolate prison? I'm terrified when I close my eyes, I'll never really leave this place even if my body is a thousand miles away. I shake my head, trying to bury the secret fear.

"What about the rest of them?" I suddenly ask, realizing how briskly we're passing by the cells.

Chloris doesn't meet my eyes. "Um-"

"We can't take them with us," Nymphora answers for her, coming from behind. "Enough talking." She brushes by me. "We have a prison to break out of."

"No." I stop, touching Chloris's hand. "We can't leave them. It's inevitable they'll go to the crystal."

She looks torn. Nymphora glares at me. I ignore her.

"I've seen what the crystal is, Chloris. It's horrible; more terrifying than you can imagine," I whisper fierce and fast. "You get *sucked* in. Your whole body melts into the crystal. You *become* a part of the crystal."

She looks horrified.

"We can't leave them." My eyes scan the corridor even as I hear Nymphora object. "There has to be a button or something to open the cell doors," I press. Our doors always opened at the same time in the morning. "There's a control room somewhere."

"This is ridiculous, Kenna!" Nymphora explodes. "We're risking our lives for people who will never do the same for us."

"We're not walking away." I look her straight in the eye.

"I know for a fact any human in there would turn me over to the Saguinox in a second," she hisses.

"Not me," I answer quietly.

"What are you ladies doing?" Kaiden rushes back to us. He gestures ahead. "Keep moving."

I shake my head. "We have to get the rest of the prisoners out."

He raises an eyebrow, but doesn't object right away like I expect him to. "That's probably going to get us killed."

"Probably, but maybe not."

He chuckles.

I'm confused.

"Danger, and a high chance of death with a flurry of blood," he muses. "All right. I'm in. "

"*What?*" Nymphora shrieks.

Chloris looks worried.

I nod. "Let's find a way to open the doors and take any who want to go with us. Do you know if they have a control room of some sort?"

"Not that I saw," he answers.

"We don't have time to go around searching for something we're not even sure is here, Kenna." Nymphora's trying to be calm.

She's right, but I can't leave. It'll haunt me forever if I do.

"Where do the guards sleep?" Chloris asks.

"On the other wing," Kaiden answers.

"I'll, um, kiss whatever guards are here, and we'll just try not to make so much noise when we break them out," Chloris suggests.

"What are we going to use to break them out?" I ask. Then, "Kaiden, is there a storage room of weapons some-where?"

"Probably, but I don't have access to it."

"So let's think about this," Nymphora's sarcastic voice breaks in. "We have no time, no access to equipment, no weapons, and no way of getting everyone to safety. Still think this is a bright idea?"

I gasp.

"What?" Chloris looks around frightfully.

"Actually, I have something that might help us," I say slowly. Turning to Kaiden, I ask, "can you take me to the caves?"

"How are Braxi crystals going to help us?"

"Braxi crystals won't help us," I reply. "But sledgeham-mers might."

CHAPTER 23

Kaiden leads us, his lean body like a beacon through a storm. I wonder how long he's been here, and why I haven't noticed him before. Even in the darkness, he doesn't hesitate, strategically walking through corridors and rooms like he's studied their interior for days. There is an antique pitcher of some kind in one room. He pretends to knock it over. We all freeze in absolute terror until he catches it before it can drop and make a sound.

"We don't have time for that!" Nymphora hisses.

Kaiden only grins at us, wiggling his eyebrows humorously.

He takes us through mostly bare and grim spaces that look similar to the cells we've been locked in.

"This building used to be a storage warehouse," he explains.

It makes sense. Each cell is small enough for someone to rent storage space.

"It was bare when the Saguinox bought it, but they didn't really bother doing much with most of it. Just the bathrooms." He gestures around. "Whatever is finished has been done by the prisoners and the Saguinox slaves. Like this room."

He opens a door.

We enter what probably had been a meeting room. I'm instantly reminded of the bath room from earlier in the day. *This must be the room for men.* Cream colors adorn every inch of space, but the décor isn't feminine. Lush paintings depict Saguinox warriors in tightly fitted metal armor defeating their enemies. A scene shows a Saguionox man standing over a headless corpse, holding the mutilated head of his opponent in one hand, and a small pale sheet in the other. Passing by, I'm offered a closer look and I take it, scrutinizing what sort of sheet he could be holding. When I realize what it is, I feel sick to my stomach.

Skin.

He's holding pieces of skin.

I look away, trying to erase the gruesome sight from my head.

Shower stalls are to the left of us, and instead of a Greek fountain there's a small sitting area with masculine chairs neatly set up side by side. There are a few wash spots where people can clean their hands and feet with scented oils.

"They haul all this stuff in their ships," Kaiden informs us. "They drop it here for the prisoners to set up. The crystal was the last thing to arrive. That's why you're digging for Braxi crystals instead of playing maid."

"All this work for a bathroom?"

"Saguinox culture values cleanliness," Kaiden answers. Chloris and Nympohora don't look interested because they probably already know this information. "Cleanliness before meals, or ceremonies, even before death. They believe in purity of the blood, body, and soul." His hand gestures to encompass the entire room. "As you can see this thought lends itself to their prisons, too."

"So they're basically alien germaphobes," I summarize.

"*Bloodthirsty* alien germaphobes," Kaiden corrects with a grin.

"Are you sure the cameras are all down?" Chloris breaks in.

"Of course. The cameras aren't here anyway," Kaiden replies, motioning us to keep moving.

I'm stunned. "They're not afraid of us at all," I say.

"No," he agrees. "This place is nothing to them. You're here because they need a couple extra workers. That's why they left you all with the guards. They've got bigger fish to fry."

What are they planning?

I feel sick inside.

"Anyway, what's there to be afraid of?" Nymphora asks. "The Saguinox are physically stronger, and they're all enhanced by the crystal. We're like mice to them." Her eyes go to my scarlet dress. "*Red* mice."

Kaiden motions us to be quiet because we're coming to a door. It's gray, like the walls beside it, and so ordinary looking I would've missed it had Kaiden not stopped us.

I move to the head of the pack right next to him. "This is the door to the outside?"

He shoots me a lopsided grin, and nods. His eyes are sparkling when he says, "Can't wait to stick it to them."

I agree. "What are you doing?" I ask.

"Shutting down the cameras and overriding their systems." I watch him punch in a few numbers before the door opens. "Like magic," he grins.

"*This* magic I'm not afraid of. It's the other magic that's frightening," I mutter, stepping out. Already the air feels less stale to me, less confined. With a shaking body, and rapid footsteps, I follow Kaiden's lead. My heart's thundering with adrenaline, and the rancid taste of fear. The night air makes me cold, but the danger of what we're doing makes me colder.

Everything feels strange, and gradually I begin to understand why. There are no animal sounds. Not even the chirping of crickets can be heard. I realize in this place that silence might be the most chilling sound of all.

In the shadows the caves ahead are the darkest part of the night. We head toward the largest cave, and the one we work in everyday. When we're standing inside the entrance, Kaiden pulls out a match from his pocket. He lights it, but it barely penetrates the blackness in front of us.

Disappointed, Kaiden says, "It's not going to be much help."

"No," I agree, sighing. "But it's better than nothing."

He holds the lit match higher as if angling it down might magnify the light.

It doesn't.

"What are we waiting for? Let's go," Nymphora urges.

"No," I object. "It's too dark. We'll be able to move faster with only two. Both of you can stay here and keep watch."

"Be quick." Chloris looks troubled.

Walking close together, Kaiden and I head deeper into the cave. "I hid some sledgehammers here. I dug up a hole and buried them."

He whistles, impressed. "How'd you manage to do that?"

I shrug, but he doesn't see it. "It's this trick I have. People don't really seem to notice me."

"Really? If I was down here, I think I'd notice you."

Remembering how easily Lenora forgot my presence, I replied, "I doubt it."

He doesn't respond. Giving me a friendly smile and a pat on the back, he says, "Lead the way."

It's difficult to see where we're going, and the darkness becomes heavier the deeper we go. I know we don't have much time, and it weighs heavily on my mind even as we agree to run ahead. Eventually, the match becomes a drop of light in an abyss of black. Ordinarily, I'd be petrified, but now I know there are scarier things than darkness.

We go down a small slope, and everything starts to feel familiar again.

I stop.

"Maybe here." I gesture in the blackness.

"Are you sure?"

I shrug. Maybe he feels it because he says, "This spot's as good as any."

We kneel, using our hands to dig. I feel like a dog searching for his bone. Kaiden holds the match over us with one hand, while maneuvering the soil below with the other. The dirt is smooth and smells metallic. I dig faster, but I don't find the hardness I expect to feel. After a few minutes, I grab Kaiden's hand, stopping him.

"It isn't here. I think we need to go further in."

He helps me up. "Just tell me where."

He intertwines his fingers with mine and I sprint ahead, knowing we're running out of time.

"Okay," I stop, breathless. "Let's try this spot." I see faint outlines of a familiar table. "It's got to be--"

The light goes out.

We freeze.

Even though I know Kaiden's here I suddenly feel completely alone. "Kaiden?"

"Yeah."

My shoulders brush against his, and I'm relieved to feel him so near me. "Hand me your light and matchbox."

"It's out."

"Let me try anyway."

His hands leave mine for a few seconds. When they return he slips something small and bulky in my palms. The matchstick is thin and coarse, and my thumb touches the head of it. Holding the matchbox with my other hand, I swipe the stick across it. The motion makes a ruffling sound, but no light appears. I try again, feeling the stick sweep across the box and scrape past my fingers.

Again, no light.

I swipe harder, feeling the head rub harder against my index finger. It creates a strange buzzing sensation, and instinctively I swipe past the matchbox and onto my skin, pressing deeper. The buzzing grows louder, and my skin feels hotter.

A cackle.

Excited, I sweep across the box one more time. It brushes against my finger--

Fire.

I hand the bright flame to Kaiden. "You just had to put some muscle into it."

He grunts.

Bending down, I feel the cold soil beneath my palm. We break the earth with as much ferocity as we can muster, moving rocks and dirt debris. My arms are tired, but I don't let up, digging with all my strength.

I'm breathing hard when Kaiden finally says, "I think this one's a false alarm."

"No." I'm stubborn. "It's here. I know it!"

I keep digging. He sighs, but continues. I don't know how long we go at it. It's probably minutes, but it feels like an hour.

After some long moments, Kaiden says, "We have to go, Kenna". His voice is gentle as if he knows how precarious I'm feeling. I pretend not to hear. "Kenna! We need to leave when it's still dark."

I stop.

Panic and guilt sprout inside me. Panic, that we've taken too much time, and guilt that we might have to leave the other prisoners after all.

Angry, I stand, stomping on the ground beside the hole we've dug. "Damn it!" I stomp again and again. It can't end this way-it just can't!

Again, my foot lands hard on the ground.

I yelp. "Ow!"

I still.

My eyes are wide when I turn to Kaiden. "It's here!" I exclaim excitedly.

He doesn't look like he believes me. I don't care though. My toes are tingling with pain, and that's proof enough for me. Kneeling for the third time, we make our hands into claws, digging furiously, knowing it's our last chance.

When my fingers finally hit metal, I let out a sigh of relief. I'm careful to move slowly, and eventually we find all four sledgehammers right on top of one another. I feel like a kid who's just found her present from Santa.

"It's amazing that you would even try to hide a weapon, but four? You're extraordinary," Kaiden says, clasping the handle of one hammer.

"Not really. Everyone knows the guards are pretty dumb." But I'm beaming with happiness.

"Let's get out of here."

We run, both of us carrying a sledgehammer in each hand. The trek back is a lot faster and Chloris is the first to see us. "What took you so long?" She sounds scared and relieved.

"I'm sorry, " I apologize, imagining the anxiety they had gone through waiting.

Nymphora's still brooding, but brightens considerably when she sees the sledgehammers. She takes one from me, testing its weight in her hands. She looks at it like it's a treasure. I'm surprised she doesn't kiss it.

"No time to play, " I tell her. "Let's go!"

We're running in the dark. My dress flows behind like a cape. I'm scared someone will see us, but the hard metal in my hands give me courage.

This time I don't need Kaiden to lead because I know where to go. I retrace our steps, going past the elaborate bathroom and through dark, dingy corridors until we reach the cells.

The dead Saguinox guard is still slumped on the floor, his face completely colorless. There's an odor emanating from his body unlike anything I've ever smelled. It's pungent and sour like rotten milk. I bend, searching him for anything valuable that might help us. All I find are cigarettes.

"What's the plan?" Chloris asks.

I look at the empty hallway in front of us, and the cells lined on each side. There are no sounds other than us, and I wonder if the other prisoners have any idea what's about to happen. "Break the locks," I reply.

"Barbaric," she comments.

"That's what they get for not even bothering to install cameras here. We're not big enough fish for them to fry," I say sarcastically, referencing Kaiden's earlier statement.

"They'll be switching guards in about ten minutes so we better hurry," he warns us.

Ten minutes?

206 · MARI ARDEN

Filled with panic, we spread out. Nymphora and Kaiden head for the cells upstairs and Chloris and I stay here. I run to the end of the hallway. I know which rooms are empty so I don't bother to stop by them. There are no handles on the doors because they're all on the inside.

I make an exasperated sound. "Do whatever you can to get it open."

The first sound of hammer hitting wood and plaster is frighteningly loud. Even though I'm prepared for it, I wince. It's the loudest sound I've ever heard here, and I have to take another deep breath to calm my shaking body.

Raising my hand, I use all my strength and bring the sledgehammer down hard on the door. The sound is harsh, but I don't stop. My hands rise up and down. Down and up. The pattern is endless, but desperation makes me resolute. Eventually, I'm able to push the first door open.

The girl inside hears the commotion. She's standing in the middle of the room, completely bewildered. The scarlet dress hangs on her skinny, malnourished body, and her eyes are as big as an owl's.

"Hi," I say, breathing hard. I pull the door all the way back. "Come on!"

I don't have time to explain so I move to the next one, hoping she understands what this means. I'm focused on getting everyone out, and it's the only thing driving me, as I pound through each door. I imagine every crack as a crack in the Saguinox plans, and it makes me push harder, and drive my hammer deeper.

Soon I feel someone next to me.

"I'm Mia," the girl says timidly. She's the prisoner from the first cell I opened.

"Go help the others," I pant.

"I want to help you."

"No--"

She pries the sledgehammer from my fingers, and I'm momentarily stunned by the strength in her little arms. Maybe she isn't so malnourished after all.

Her small body heaves with exertion, but her swings are strong. Other prisoners are walking around dazed, confused or in tears. It's as if I'm in the aftermath of a war zone where everyone is quiet and shocked.

Someone grabs me.

Chloris's eyes are wide when she looks at me. I can see people behind her. Some are running. One's trying to break open a door with a chair, and another has Chloris's hammer, pounding on another door with as much strength as she can muster.

"We have to go."

I start to shake my head.

"We've done all that we can. We have to go!"

She pulls me, and I'm too weak to fight her. Kaiden and Nymphora are waiting for us. I see a second guard lying nearby in a pool of blood.

"We got two minutes before the system turns back on," Kaiden says. "The alarm will ring when we leave. That should create enough of a distraction for the rest of them to get out."

A female prisoner runs by carrying his or Nymphora's sledgehammer. He grabs her. "There's another exit through that hallway!" He shouts. "Take the others and run!" He doesn't wait for her to answer.

For the second time that night we sprint through the prison. It's surreal to run through it again. This time my heart is lighter, knowing more might survive, too.

Someone will get out and tell what happened here. This suffering won't be for nothing.

The exit door is up ahead.

I take a deep breath.

The second we bolt through it the alarm sounds. It's a siren, squealing in our ears. It hurts to listen, and we plunge forward. The air that greets us is harsh and un-yielding. Manic shrilling from the bell we triggered surrounds us, alerting everyone to what we've done.

The fence is up ahead, about thirty feet away, but every inch feels like a block.

Kaiden reaches it first, almost sliding to get near it. His skin touches the electricity, but he's unfazed. He fumbles with something from his pockets. A scissor. Or at least it appears to look like one.

Nymphora is talking, but the alarm is deafening. It's the only thing I hear in my head. She looks as desperate as I feel. Kaiden examines the tool, quickly turning it over.

I'm not sure what he's doing, but my heart's bursting out of my chest. Silently, I count to keep from falling to the ground.

Kaiden's fingers grasp the scissor.

One.

He opens it, ready to cut the wires.

Two.

He positions the blades between the electric cable.

Boom.

CHAPTER 24

Blood.

It smells like I'm drenched in it. I try to swallow but I can't. The taste is in my mouth. I can't tell if it's mine or if it belongs to someone else. Maybe both.

My eyes are trying to adjust in the dark, but spots of white and orange flutter across my vision. Disorientated, my fingers clutch at the ground beneath me, feeling the soft soil. Trying to discern where I am, I lift my hand. Nothing. I can't feel anything there. Terror ripples through me.

Taking a deep breath, I inhale in debris and ash. Immediately, I begin coughing. The movement hurts my chest, and my feeble body jerks in a spasm. I try to speak, but nothing comes out. My fingers dig deeper into the ground, desperate to move, desperate to feel *anything*. But there's only a void.

Motionless, I realize I'm lying down. Maybe I'm staring at the sky, but all I see are spots too bright to be real. A deafening silence roars in my ears. It's an unnatural kind of quiet. My body is numb, but my mind is beginning to stir. The last thing I remember is Kaiden cutting the wires. Like a movie, snippets play in my head: going into the caves, trying to free the prisoners, and an alarm shrieking.

A loud boom shakes the ground I lie on. As if on cue, every part of me suddenly becomes alive. Nerve endings tingle, and I let out a guttural sound. Arching my back, I strain to breathe clean air amidst the debris floating into my mouth. When I'm breathing again, the first thing I do is look at my trembling body. I'm covered in dirt and blood. My dress is drenched in soil and body fluids darken the once scarlet color into an almost black one. My chest hurts, but it isn't my lungs that make me ache. My skin's cut, and I notice bruises and scrapes covering my arms and legs, too.

"Holy crap." My shocked whisper barely drifts into the night before a loud sound shoots past it, violently surprising me. It sounds like gunfire. Alert and in pain, I know I have to move. I'm on the ground with nowhere to hide and nothing to hide with. Trying to crawl, I attempt to roll over. It takes a few tries, but the sounds of more gunfire motivate me to keep struggling.

I'm crawling through a war zone. Even though I don't see any bodies, there are debris, holes, and other materials like glass on the ground. Some parts are covered in smoke, and when I pass through it I cover my mouth. The smell is sickeningly sweet, and I'm petrified it's filled with poison.

One knee is bloody with the ground pressing into it. I want to walk, but I'm afraid I'll be seen. My vision's still spotty, but eventually I see grass and bushes. The prison walls loom ahead, covered by a faint cloud of smoke. Vague memories of Kaiden putting something on the fence to disable the electricity drift into my mind.

There's a part up ahead where a piece of land broke, sliding under as if something has collapsed beneath it. I crawl there, hiding behind part of a tree. The gunshots sound even louder here, and I wonder if I've moved myself nearer. There's no time to change though because an earsplitting boom explodes in the sky, and I crouch, trying to protect my head with my hands. Gravel and other debris fall on me. It's so thick I choke. Curling myself into a tighter ball, I find it's impossible to shield myself from the torrent of soil, ash, and sticks, but I try anyway. Glass and thorns scrape my skin. I wince, but I don't move, riding out the waves like a vulnerable seed in the wind.

It's over in less than a minute. When it's done, my ears are numb, and I hear sounds as distant echoes. *I can't stay here.* Checking my surroundings, I try to analyze my next move. If I climb over, it will only bring me back to the Saguinox and probable death.

I'm on the edge of a very small field, but beyond that trees and dense shrubbery surround this place. Making the only decision I can, I go to my right where the trees are heaviest. Crouching on wobbly feet, I note I'm about fifty feet away. It's not far, but right now it feels like miles. Something burns, and I'm sure I've stepped on a piece of glass somewhere. My feet and body are completely bare, with the exception of my flimsy dress, but I don't feel the night chill. Adrenaline filled panic and heat from the thunderous explosions wash over me, giving me an electric high that keeps me moving when I know I shouldn't be.

Slipping past the lopsided tree like a ghost, I move as fast as I can, not daring to look anywhere but ahead. I don't know how many Saguinox are out there, and I don't want to find out. It's hard, but I try to run. My bare feet press against jagged rocks and uneven ground, but I tell myself the pain is nothing. Survival is everything. Pressing ahead, I ignore thorns from thick shrubbery. I hear a sound and I still, completely frozen. My heart's beating as loud as the gunshots.

"Kenna." The voice is hoarse, filled with pain.

"Chloris?" I whisper in the dark, a sudden relief filling me.

"Right here." She sounds like she's next to me. Searching, I see nothing but leaves.

"Where?"

Something soft touches my shoulder, and I jump back. "Here," she answers.

I blink, as understanding dawns. Parts of her face are visible like her eyes, and her swollen mouth, but everything else is hidden, camouflaged by the night and her body.

"You're a tree," I state the obvious, dumbfounded to see her in her other form.

"Sort of. It's camouflage," she replies, wincing. "Can you get off my leg?"

"Oh. Sorry." I move, shifting my weight to my other foot. She's still cringing though so I ask, "Where are you hurt?"

"Everywhere. Burns. Scrapes." She closes her eyes in pain, breathing hard. "I was thrown in the air. I think I have a couple broken ribs, and the explosion did something to my body," she whispers. "Kenna, I can feel parts of my powers returning, but I can't open them. I hurt all over."

"Did they bomb us?"

"I think so. Either that or they've hidden explosives everywhere. Probably both."

"Where are Nymphora and Kaiden?" With alarm, my eyes search around Chloris, but I see nothing. "Where?"

She doesn't answer, but she shakes her head, the same trepidation reflected on her face.

"I was behind you, and then I was thrown over there." Her head jerks forward in the direction I came from. "I crawled over and hid here."

"How long ago?"

"Ten minutes, maybe less. I was knocked out good."

"They're here somewhere. They have to be. We'll find them." I promise, not willing to think of a different alternative. "There are trees everywhere. They're just hidden somewhere." I break off as I see the expression on her face.

Her eyes are open and she's staring dazedly at me. I step nearer. They're glazed looking and glossy. Her body has a brownish tint to it that makes her look deceptively like a tree. Yet, this close I can smell burnt flesh and rotting skin.

"Chloris," I try to shake her gently, but firmly so she'll look at me. "We're going to get out of here." Her skin's strangely dry and ashy. Slowly, her eyes roll up, and I can see the startling whites against her green face. "I'm not leaving without you, Chloris!"

She can't hear me anymore. Seeing the expression on her face, I grab her before she abruptly falls. Any ounce of power she might have been using vanishes. Putting her arm over my shoulder, I stand with her. Real terror drums through me. I have no idea where we are, no powers to speak of, and Chloris is putting all her weight on me, unable to move on her own.

Unexpectedly, searchlights shine around us and I know the Saguinox are out there looking. Waiting.

A bullet whizzes past me.

"Duck, Chloris!" I shriek. When I crouch, her body goes down with me. Her eyes are completely closed now, and I'm petrified she's lost consciousness from the pain. Seemingly out of nowhere, lightning flashes across the sky, followed by a raucous rumbling.

"Haven't you heard? Escape is an illusion."

CHAPTER 25

The voice is close, and I freeze, motionless. It's a voice I've never heard before. It's breathy and low, filled with a Saguinox accent that makes me fear the unknown.

"We have a friend of yours."

For an endless moment, I feel completely trapped. What does he mean? Nymphora and Kaiden's faces flash in my mind in snippets. Suddenly I'm picturing them hurt, and in pain, at the mercy of a Saguinox guard. Clutching Chloris's arm tightly, I attempt to maneuver us further back. I try to be silent, but her dead weight is impossible to conceal, and the leaves hiding us rustle like bells.

Laughter rings out, and his voice is amused. "Do you really think you can hide?" His accent punctures each word, emphasizing it like a stabbing dagger. "I smell you. Do you know that? I hear your beating heart. I can taste your perfect fear." He makes a satisfied sound, as if he's sampled something delicious. "Death's waiting." He speaks those words in whisper, a sick awe lacing his smooth tone.

A psycho alien! Somehow I know we're in for it now.

"Do you know what I do to little humans like you?" he asks, the low rumble of his voice sending chills through my already frozen skin. I push Chloris further back. A light rain is beginning to fall, and every drop sticks to her like syrup. Trying to ignore it, I frantically place leaves and other plant parts over her body. Her swollen red lips are the last part of her I can see, and I place a large leaf over it until she's completely disappeared.

I hear a loud shrieking and the wind picks up. Before I can blink, everything around us begins to crumble. Leaves, shrubs and trees are literally breaking before my very eyes. The trunk of a tree next to me falls, and I move back to avoid it, but before I do that it shatters into dust. A thousand leaves collapsing and disintegrating into brown powder drown my scream out.

Something hits me, and I'm flying. It feels like an invisible hand is pulling me, and shooting my body across the sky. All I see is smoke, and blackened earth before I'm stopped, suspended in mid air. My legs are flailing helplessly for an unbearable amount of time, then my body violently turns, viciously jerked back toward the ground. Plummeting down faster than a fireball, I choke on my own vomit as the force of whatever he's doing pushes the contents of my stomach up into my throat. The ground is hard when I finally fall, and something inside my leg snaps, breaking into a dozen parts.

His laughter is louder than my howl of pain, and all I hear is the echo of his cackle as a throbbing pain centers itself on my whole right side. Looking down, my ankle is turned at a frightening angle. Unable to bear the intense throbbing, I clutch it, feeling bones that shouldn't be there protruding against my skin.

Hearing him behind me, I look back. Another blue flash of lightening fills the sky, creating a halo of light around the beautiful creature. He's dressed like a medieval prince. A fitted metal chest piece is wrapped around him like a cloth. He has on dark pants protected by metal plates.

He's covered in blood.

He's dragging something behind him. At first I think it's a bag, but when I stare harder I realize it's too large. He's hauling it effortlessly, wrapping gleaming chains around his fingers. Almost instantly, wisps of dark hair come into sight, and I gasp.

She's a prisoner. The one I'd released earlier. Mia.

My stomach drops.

There are metal chains around her neck, and he's using it as a leash, dragging her weak body through the mud. Her hands claw at the restraint, trying to breathe, but he only pulls her harder, wrapping the chains tighter.

"I hear there are *prisoners* are trying to escape. That's never happened before. No one's ever been that stupid." He grins, showing white teeth. "It's my duty to rid this world of stupid people. It looks like we'll start with you two."

Suddenly, I recognize his face. "You're Damien, the ambassador," I say, almost accusingly. The merciless countenance looking at me now bears almost no resemblance to the angelic face flashed on television for weeks. After everything I know about the Saguinox I'm not surprised, but for some reason I still feel betrayed.

"Yes," he confirms.

"Why are you doing this?" I ask, my voice more feeble than I want it to be.

"There's a war brewing, and I'm afraid you're on the wrong side of it. Earth will be our home now."

I shake my head. "You can't have our planet."

His smile doesn't reach his eyes. "I'm afraid it's already too late. Now," he says with deadly calm. "Where are the rest of them?"

Has everyone escaped? A flutter of hope spreads through my chest.

"I don't know what you're talking about."

"No?" He looks impatient. "Fine. Maybe you need a little incentive." He points to Mia, who looks terrified. "Her life will depend on you." Fear grips my heart. Without taking his eyes off me, he lifts a hand. Mia jerks upward, held up by an invisible rope. Seeing him do magic momentarily shocks me.

"I can make this hurt. A lot. And I can make it last a very long time. For both of you." He pauses. "Where are the others?" His voice is deadly soft, and instinctively I flinch. He waits patiently, pointing to Mia, ready to show more magic. Breathing hard, I try to come up with a plan, but all I can think about is pain and what will happen if I can't figure this out.

"Nothing?"

I'm frantic. "Wait! Please! I- I really don't know--"

His growl of impatience drowns out my words. With a flick of his wrist Mia glides to him, a foot off the ground. Her body is moving at an odd angle, and as she comes closer I see something is pulling her skin forward. It's like Damien has hooks on every inch of her body. She's jerking, making terrifying sounds of pain. Every move she attempts to make only brings her more torture. As she nears, her skin is stretched further from her body until I can see blood. At first it's just a trickle, but as she makes her way to his side, scarlet liquid cascade down like a waterfall. Damien snaps his fingers, disturbingly excited. Skin from the left front of her face rip off, crumbling like eggshells.

I hear two voices screaming. When one abruptly stops, I realize the other abnormal shrieking sounds are coming from me. I tell myself to stop, but I can't. I see bones, and muscle, and mutilated flesh. I smell her pain and it's filled with the scent of metal and blood. Damien's other hand rises, slowly curling into a fist. As his hands coil inward, I feel an invisible hand squeezing my throat. It silences me, and all sounds stop.

"That's better," he says, turning toward me. " Now that you understand, every minute that you waste more skin will come off."

He's continuing to talk but the only thing I hear is the pounding of my own heart. I want to tell him that he's suffocating me, but his invisible grip on my throat is tight and unyielding. Deprived of air, my body panics. Damien's face starts to blur. Slowly, I see his glowing eyes slowly merge into one. I try to take another breath, but I can't.

All I can think is that this is the end.

Remember.

I shiver.

Do you remember the stars, Kenna? the voice whispers. It sounds like Rhys, and Kaiden, and Nymphora and even Chloris. It sounds like every voice I've ever heard. *Do you remember how you burned brighter than every single sun?*

In my mind I can see it: an inferno. Giant waves of fire are building. Abruptly, I'm hot, so very hot. In my head the blaze is growing, becoming combustion of reds and blues that devour every shadow attempting to escape. I feel dizzy, and everything hurts. I want to lie down forever.

Listen, Kenna. A new voice is speaking. It's soft and comforting. The sounds of the fire abruptly dim in my mind, and the images I see move in slow motion. She continues to speak over them, like a distant echo.

Or a far more distant memory.

I love you, Kenna, but I will never be there for you. I know you can hear me. I know you're listening. I've done something very bad. It's the only way to protect you. I've made you weak. I hope you are weak forever, my love.

I can hear her heartbeat like I'm inside her body. Her voice becomes muffled because I can hear her other organs, too.

If there is ever a time when you need to be strong, I want you to rise, and I want you to fight. I want you to become everything we hoped you wouldn't be. And when you are at your last breath, promise me you'll burn... you'll burn until every part of you is on fire.

Quietly her voice fades, calling for a blaze. It stays in my head, and echoes in my body. In my mind I can see a fireball forming. It's gathering flames, encircling the colors into an inferno. I can feel it in my soul, rushing and pulsing trying to reach an outlet.

When I can breathe no more, I burst into flames.

Chapter 26

I hear the snapping sounds first.

Repetitive and fast, they're an undercurrent to the screams. Immediately, the taut grip on my throat loosens, and the invisible hand burns. I hear a low growl of pain, and something heavy drops.

When I open my eyes, I see Mia's pale body, lying completely still on the ground. Bruised skin and muscle hang out. Gagging, I cover my mouth to stop the vomit from rising. Damien hisses, clutching his hands. They're smoking, and a slight sizzling sound is heard.

"Fire," he says with awe, staring at the smoke on his hand. Abruptly he looks at me with glee, making his handsome face crazed. "Do it again!" he urges in a low fanatical voice. He tries to move closer.

Quickly, I put my hand up. "Don't!" I shout. "I'll- I'll burn you!"

"That's the idea."

My hand remains up, warning him to stay back.

Damien's eyes concentrate on my palm with rising intensity. Thin curls of smoke rise from it. I want to press my hand against the cool ground underneath me, but I'm too afraid to try. His glowing eyes suddenly widen with shock. "The mark," he whispers. "That's where the fire crystal was first placed on you, burned into your body." His eyes rake down the length of me, devious and hungry.

It's enough to make me snap. I picture an orange blaze shooting from my hand, and with a burst of force, I unleash it. He yells, jumping back, but it's too late. My fire scorches part of his left side.

I'm stunned.

"Oh yeah," he says as if he's in ecstasy. "Here. We. *Go!*"

He jumps, soaring up.

Something ancient comes over me. My mind is numb from fear and shock, but my body is flawless, sprouting something fierce from my body. Somehow I aim for him, shooting an array of fire. It's coming out like a flood of stars. Waves of energy pour through me, and despite my injuries I feel more powerful than ever. I think about every person lost to the crystal, and the desperation of the other prisoners, and a rage greater than anything I've ever felt consumes me.

He comes at me fast, and when I blink his fist connects with my jaw. I see black spots when my face hits the hard earth. His hands grab my hair, and he twists the strands into his fist, creating a tight ball. He jerks me up, and I fly ahead, landing in a heap on the ground.

I touch my head, feeling as if it's been sliced open. My fingers stroke a thick wetness that can only be blood. I feel a few bald spots, and even from the distance I can see strands of brown intertwined in his fingers, flailing in the wind.

"The first crystal we took was over a century ago," he tells me, drawing nearer. "The water crystal. The carrier was a girl like you. She was a dwarf and she hid here on earth, thinking this place would keep her safe from us. But it didn't. Our prince found and annihilated her." He pauses, watching me struggle as I try to get up. "The second crystal, air was found ten years after from a healer. He begged us to spare his family. He tried to hide them, but we found every single person that mattered to him, and we let him watch as they died. Slowly. We thought that would show the universe no one can hide from us."

He's almost to me now, and I crawl back. My hand is hot, like I've been electrocuted and my whole palm is black.

"Thirty years ago we found the third crystal, tierra. A shape shifter had it. A *plant* shape shifter." He laughs. "Needless, to say we took *that* one with ease. We proved there is nothing and no one stronger than us." He stops. Abruptly an angry look comes over his face. "Imagine our surprise when we were told someone had been keeping a secret from us. Someone had hid the fire crystal."

Damien is next to me now, and his hand lashes out, gripping my neck. I think of fire, and both my hands clutch his arm, fiercely trying to burn him. The metal is sizzling, melting in my hands, but his grip stays firm.

He's looking into my eyes, and abruptly his go black. He's searching my mind, and Chloris' warning comes back to me. *He digs into your mind, and pulls out your darkest fears, then he makes it come to life. Your heart, your mind, your body, your soul, dies. Every part of you dies.* Unable to move, I stare at him, hypnotized. Dark blue mists form, and I glimpse the sheer sapphire fog from the corner of my eye. Pungent, it smells like a sweet poison. Almost in slow motion, it drifts into my nostrils, teasing softly before floating. When it touches me, I'm blinded by azure colors, surrounded by smells I can't place. He's searching in my memories, and the first pull from his mind makes me dizzy. Many pictures flicker in the fog like flashing lights. It's as if I'm watching multiple cameras at once, and my whole life is literally passing before my eyes. The iridescent images are moving so fast my stomach feels like I'm on a roller coaster ride. It heaves with each new picture, but I'm motionless, suspended in Damien's grip. He finds what he's looking for because all the other picture screens suddenly disappear until a single one is left. It sprints to the front.

Murky water flickers on and off. Flying above the ocean, I suddenly remember this memory. Unable to control myself I scream, but it's quickly cut off when I'm brutally pulled into the image. Flying head first, I plunge into the cold water. Before I can move, a dark weight lands on me, pressing me down. Drowning me. Suffocating me.

Even though I'm dying in my mind, Damien's breath is hot on my cheek. Unable to move, I whimper helplessly in terror. "A little fire doesn't scare me, girl," he whispers.

"Maybe this will," a masculine voice retorts.

I hear something vibrating, and the weight on me freezes. Suddenly, the darkness disappears, and my body jerks out, pushing through water and blue mists, back into my own mind.

When I open my eyes Damien is frozen on top of me. His pupils are no longer black. He's still, completely motionless. For a moment I feel a second of deep relief and bottomless terror as I gaze into his manic face. Someone pushes him off me. I'm so relieved I start crying.

Kaiden gathers me in his arms, clutching my body tightly. " It's all right, Kenna," he tells me softly, his face in my hair. He embraces me for many seconds. He pulls back, holding my face in his hands. "This only freezes him for a few minutes. We have to go *now!*" He notices the way my body is twisted, and maneuvers around it, pulling me up. Half carrying and half dragging me, Kaiden pushes through thorn and trees, and into a forest.

"Chloris!" I manage to yell out, narrowly avoiding a low hanging branch. I grit through the pain of attempting to run with a broken ankle.

"Nymphora's taking care of her," he replies, not breaking his speed. I'm trying to follow him, but everything feels so excruciating that I cry out, falling to the ground. Something sharp slits my cheek.

"My ankle's broken," I confess tearfully.

Without breaking his stride, he hauls me over his shoulders, breaking leaves and branches to do it. *No*, I try to tell him, *you can't carry me* and *run*. But I'm so relieved to be putting pressure off my leg that all I can do is grasp him tighter.

Within minutes I hear a terrifying sound behind us. Looking up from Kaiden's neck, I brush past thick leaves. One moment I feel the rough texture against my forehead, and the next it's gone, fading into brown ashes. Blinking, my arms reach out for the trunk of a squatting tree. The barest touch from my fingertips releases its death, and the tree crumbles, breaking into a hundred pieces.

"Shit!" Kaiden yells, seeing what just happened. "What the hell *is* this place?"

"Escape is an illusion," I whisper more to myself than him. "He will find us." The Saguinox warning passes through my lips like a poison. "He uses our fears against us," I inform Kaiden, recalling what Chloris confided. "Chloris told me he sucks our life and our soul."

He doesn't say anything, but his body shivers.

I feel a bubble of sadness burst, wetting me with the inevitable.

"Kaiden," I say his name, depressed and resolute. "We can't run. We have to face him." My voice breaks. "Kaiden!" I shout louder, when he begins to move faster. "Stop. Just stop." He doesn't, but maybe he hears something in my voice because he slows down.

My heart is hammering, and I hear it in my ears when I spot Damien. He's in the distance, jumping and soaring like a magical predator. Soon he will be next to us. I look around, frantic for a plan.

"What's your power?" I shout to Kaiden as the wind starts to pick up.

"Don't have any."

"You're *human?*"

"Sort of," he replies. "Mostly."

I shake my head, too anxious to sort out what he means. "I have fire."

"What?"

"I can shoot out fire with my body. Something about a crystal..." Unexpectedly, he stops, nearly dropping me.

"What did you say?" His voice is quiet, and I'm not sure if he's happy about my power or if he's upset. Just thinking the word *power* brings shivers down my spine. It still feels so unreal I almost want to use it again, just to prove it to Kaiden and myself. He sets me down on my feet, gazing at me with a look I can't decipher.

"What did you say?"

Impulsively, I show him my birthmark, remembering what Damien had said. He touches my palm, holding it like a piece of china. "Is this where it entered you?"

I'm assuming by "it" he means the fire crystal. "I don't know. Damien thought so."

"How long have you known?" he demands, angry.

"Maybe fifteen minutes."

His face tightens. "Crap, Kenna! I can't teach you how to use your powers now! It takes a lifetime to master it!"

I glare at him, almost regretting I told him. Before I can make a smartass retort, every single plant around us shatters like glass. Within seconds Kaiden and I are out in the open as vulnerable prey. He curses, grabbing me.

"Let's go!" He tries to carry me, but I resist, pushing his hands away.

"No! We can't outrun him, not with me injured. We have to face him, Kaiden."

He looks unhappy.

I can see him thinking in his head. I almost wish he would say "no", and think of something brilliant. His eyes are darting around, searching for an escape route. When his eyes go back to Damien's sprinting form, I see his lips tighten in resolution. Every ounce of hope disintegrates, and I try to stand taller, even though I feel small inside.

Kaiden pushes me behind him. "Do exactly as I say. I might not have a power the way that you do, but I know a lot about magic."

Damien is plowing through, destroying everything in his path.

Fear overwhelms me.

"From what I know about Saguinox warriors, they all have a killing power. If Chloris is right, he will need to get into our minds and take our fears out. We need to keep moving so he doesn't get a chance to do that." Kaiden is talking fast, trying to explain everything as rapidly as he can. "He will probably try to take me down first, and take the crystal from you last. I'll distract him, and you use your powers to kill him."

Kill. An apprehensive shiver goes down my spine. "Yes," I agree, but I'm trembling so hard Kaiden looks back at me, worried.

His face softens. "Hey, you're the only one in this universe with a crystal. Your magic knows no bounds. You can and you *will* defeat him." I really don't understand what he's saying, yet, something in his eyes captivates me. Kaiden looks at me like he believes every word. His confidence gives me a desperate surge of strength, but it also makes me want to puke.

"All right, here he comes, Kenna," Kaiden warns, completely hiding me with his body. For a split second I'm safe, and then everything around me erupts.

I scream as the ground starts to rumble.

"Shit!" Kaiden curses.

Damien runs toward us, and Kaiden braces himself before jumping up, meeting him halfway. They both fall to the ground with a *thud.* Limping to the side, I try to follow them. Kaiden doesn't have a power, but he's strong. He takes every punch Damien delves him, and reciprocates it back just as violently. The wind and rain play together in a fierce dance, urging their aggression on. Curling my fists, I close my eyes imagining a dozen perfect arrows, filled with venomous fire. Swiftly raising my hands, I aim. The arrows appear from thin air, gathering in front of me. With a grunt, I push them forward. They fly, some hitting the ground and others hitting both Damien and Kaiden.

The fire hits Kaiden first and I hear him shout. He's violently flipped to his back. I scream when his head hits the ground. A loose arrow plunges Damien from behind and he screeches, arching his head toward the sky. It's a death cry, and desperation fills me as I plunge ahead.

Damien pulls the arrow from his back. For a moment his palms glow, and he breaks it in half. Instantly, the broken arrow disappears.

Mid- stride, I recoil back in shock, uncertain of what to do next. My palms are aching, but I lift them anyway, discharging as much fire as I can, aiming for Damien. Seeing Damien's exposed neck, Kaiden takes his chance, seizing him by the throat. Damien is too fast though, and in less than a second they both are suffocating each other. Damien is trying to stare into Kaiden's eyes, attempting to bring his greatest fear to life.

"No!" I move as fast as I can, shooting fire. The pain is so intense my arm might fall off at any second. With his other hand Damien stops me in mid-stride, his invisible grip holding me in place. My fire stops, frozen.

Abruptly, Kaiden stops struggling, gazing at Damien, transfixed.

"No!" The grasp on my neck tightens. Something small and bright catches my eyes, and I look up. A star. A single star. Shutting my eyes tight, I picture a burning star. I give it a multitude of colors, red, orange, and blues. I make it into a moving fireball, rotating and turning like waves churning. When I open my eyes again, it emerges in front of me, faint at first, and harder and brighter as I hold the picture in my head. My hands grab the invisible rope on my neck, and I see all my fingers are flaming red. Burning the rope with my fingers, I gaze into the fiery star, silently commanding it to devour the alien. When the rope slowly loosens, melting underneath my on-

slaught, I shout with every ounce of energy I have left:
"Go!"

With a roar, the flaming star sends itself through the
short distance to Damien. It launches itself onto his back,
thick like liquid cement. Cackling, the fire melts the
metal on his body. With a shout, Damien jumps off
Kaiden, flailing his arms wildly to put it out. The rain is
steadily coming stronger, but it's no match for my fire,
and the star burns brighter, consuming more.

Kaiden looks dazed on the ground, staring at Damien's
burning form. I limp to him, tugging his shirt. "Kaiden!
Let's go!" It takes a moment, but he seems to snap out of
his haze. He shakes his head like he's trying to get rid of
something in his head, and takes my hand. Damien is
howling, and still alive. I want to go back to finish him.

I don't get my chance though because something is
suddenly roaring from underneath me.

"Watch out!"

CHAPTER 27

The earth is breaking, shuddering to be free. I scream, clutching Kaiden. He's trembling violently, and all of a sudden I know I'm too late. Damien has already pulled out his greatest fear.

"What is it?" I shout to Kaiden over the earsplitting roars.

"A night creature."

I have no idea what that is, but I know it's not good because Kaiden's face is paper white.

"If I kill Damien, will it die too?"

"I-I- don't know." Kaiden looks at the ground, violently anticipating what will come out. I look back to Damien, and my star is still devouring him, slowly burning through his skin. He's still standing though, and I feel a rush of panic. Should I leave Kaiden to finish off Damien? Looking at the petrified expression on Kaiden's face I'm afraid if I leave he'll be unable to protect himself. My heart is pounding with my decision.

"Kaiden!" I grab his face, pulling it down to me. "Kaiden!"

His eyes are completely round and unblinking. I don't know what else to do so I kiss him. The kiss is a wet and desperate one. It tastes like rain and panic, and when his cold mouth moves against mine, I know I've made the right choice. I pull away, gasping for breath. His eyes are no longer dazed and he's looking at me with a shocked expression.

"I'm going to kill Damien. You stay back and kick some night creature butt!" Saying the words "night creature" seems to make him nervous again, but he's looking at me strangely like he's suddenly seeing me for the first time. He nods, then pulls me roughly into his arms and gives me another quick kiss. I let him, hoping it will make him stronger. When I pull away again, I see that his eyes are back to normal.

"Go!" he shouts.

I limp back to Damien. He's still standing and it's a grotesque sight to behold. His skin is burning, some parts are scorched black, and others an odd muddy brown. His eyes continue to glow though, and when he spots me, he snarls, the sound vibrating through the flames still latched to him. I picture more arrows and I shoot them toward him. There is less this time because my energy has waned considerably, and he dodges them, raising his hand to take hold of me. I know this trick already so I fall to the ground, crawling and dodging his invisible arms. My leg is breaking more underneath the pressure of what I'm doing, but I don't dare stop. When I get close enough

I use every part of my body to stand. I make a flaming fist and punch him in the face. Simultaneously his hand connects with my cheek, slamming me back. It's got a trace of fire on it, and my skin sizzles with the contact. Within seconds, my face is numb.

I shove him back, and my leg collapses underneath me. Falling back with him, I grunt with the impact of our bodies. We crumple in a struggling heap, our magic spinning between us. Even in his state, his eyes are slowly growing black, and I panic. Clutching his shirt tightly, my hands turn into flames.

His screams of agony don't stop his powers though, and I feel him touching my mind. Desperately, I raise two fiery fingers and press them into Damien's eyes, digging as deep as I can. His howls of pain terrify me, but I don't stop, pushing harder until I feel the muscles underneath his eye sockets. Then I twist, shoving more fire into his face with my fingers. I don't stop digging until he's completely collapsed on top of me.

When I finally realize his face is next to mine, I scream, pushing his body away. The flames are still licking him, and they swirl around him, latching like maggots. I watch, fascinated I created that, but disgusted at the same time. My fingers are wet with blood, mucous, and fire.

A loud howl sounds close by, making me flinch. Turning toward Kaiden, I see a giant black wolf like creature circling him, red eyes glaring menacingly. It's larger than he is. Dread fills my body as I struggle to get up. Emitting low growls, the gigantic creature is digging his claws into the ground, baring large fangs the size of my arm. Kaiden is bracing himself, holding his hands up like a boxer.

Reaching over I grab some flames, decaying by Damien's body. I let it wash over me, massaging for more fire. I curl my fists, stretching my fingers to pull for more flames. I'm so tired that at first nothing comes out then gently, more fire is created, pulsing on the surface of my skin.

Crouching the creature roars, jumping onto Kaiden. His long nails slash Kaiden's chest. When I see his blood spilling out, I want to faint. Screaming as loud as I can to get its attention, I yell, "Over here you piece of filth! Over here!"

Fighting to get up, I use the ground to push my body. I crawl over. The distance isn't far, but my body is so ravaged I can barely move. Trying to shoot the fire, I raise my hands but it's no use. The blaze sputters, but continues to rest on my fingers.

"Kaiden!" I shout. "Bring it over here!"

He spares me a look like I'm crazy, and continues to ward off the creatures biting advances. *Damn it,* I think, crawling over. The animal's jaws snap precariously close to Kaiden's face, and it's enough to give me the energy to crawl faster. My bleeding knees are drenched in water and soil. Through sheer determination, or desperation, Kaiden flips the animal to its side, and both struggle to dominate. Kaiden punches with all his might, narrowly avoiding sharp claws and teeth.

When I'm near, he catches my eyes, and tries to push the animal closer. That's all I need, and reaching my hand out, I pour every ounce of fire left in my body onto the animal.

It howls, screeching. It's the most terrifying sound I've ever heard, and I'm so afraid I press my hands deeper into the fur, transferring more flames onto its flesh. Kaiden pushes the creature further from his body, and closer to me. When I can't hear any more grotesque screams from the animal, I pull my hand back, staring at the blackness stained there.

Breathing hard, Kaiden stands up, looking as disheveled and exhausted as I am. Walking over to me, he gives me his hands. I take it and he helps me up, arms over my waist. He looks to Damien's smoking body, then to the beast burning in front of us.

"First thing you should know: magical creatures take forever to die."

A tiny smile curls the corner of my lips. We're both staring at each other with identical expressions of bafflement at what we've just survived. Even though Kaiden's holding me, I sway, dizzy. Looking at him helplessly, my whole body collapses. When I close my eyes, I'm thinking nothing at all.

CHAPTER 28

Something soft touches my face. I wrinkle my nose to chase it away, which makes me sneeze. Jerking awake, I try swatting the insect back. When I do, my hand smacks straight on to a hard chest.

Kaiden's hard chest.

Suddenly, everything comes rushing back to me. Escape. The explosion. Damien. Kaiden. Death.

Fire.

With that last thought, I abruptly straighten.

"Ow!" we both yell simultaneously as my head bumps into Kaiden's chin. Feeling the arms around me sway slightly, I grasp his neck for more support.

"Sorry."

"It's ok," he says, but he's cringing. I know it's from more than just me. We've had quite a night.

"Kaiden, you can put me down." I shift anxiously in his arms. "I want to try walking." Gently, he unlaces the hand around my knees, setting me softly on my feet. The second my weight is put on my right leg, I cringe, shud-

dering from the impact. Gritting my teeth, I try to re-
move myself from Kaiden's hold, but he's firm, pressing
his fingers into my back.

"Let me help you." When I open my mouth to protest,
he continues. "I need to. Or else we'll never get out of
this place." It takes a moment, but I finally nod, conced-
ing his better judgment. Feeling like a big baby, I let him
take me into his arms again, listening to the steady
rhythm of his gait.

It's still dark out. "How long have we been walking?"

"A couple hours."

A couple hours? He's not breathing very hard." Aren't
you tired?"

"Yes," he admits.

Bewildered, I remark, "You sure don't sound like it."

I feel him shrug. "I have a larger energy reserve than
most do. It's sort of left over residue from my ancestry."

"Oh?" My interest piqued, I ask, "What does that
mean?"

"It means I come from a long line of magic, which is
ironic because I don't actually *have* any magic." He
chuckles, and I feel the vibrations through my sides. I settle my head deeper into his body.

"Does that upset you?"

He takes a moment to think, then answers candidly,
"No. It actually doesn't. I think who you are matters more
than what magic you have." He sounds serious and wise.

I smile into his shirt. "And who are you, Kaiden?" I ask
softly, realizing I don't know much about the guy who
helped save my life.

"I'm an earthling like you. I was born and raised here. A lot of us are," he confesses, grinning. "We've been here for thousands of years, living and hiding among you." He hums the X-Files theme song, and I laugh, looking up into his face. He's gazing ahead so he doesn't notice me studying him, observing the dimpled chin and strong nose. From underneath him I can see thick eye lashes framing electric blue eyes. I'm so close I can actually see wisps of dark blonde hair growing above his lips.

Suspicious, I ask, "Are you naturally a red head?" Instantly, he looks embarrassed.

Hiding a smile, I say, "No judgment here. I tell myself it's real even if it comes from a bottle," I half joke.

He grins. "Is it that obvious?"

"Well I'm literally an inch from your face." For some reason that seems to make him happy and he presses his head closer until we're centimeters apart. I hold my breath, suddenly reminded of the reckless kiss I shared with him earlier. Any other time I would be mortified, but tonight I feel different from myself. I still feel fear and pain, but my heart's feeling something else as well: stalwart. Strong.

Dangerous.

It's just a little bit of power, but it's enough to put something forceful in my eyes.

"All right," he says, looking mischievous. "I'll show you mine if you show me yours."

"Are we talking about the same thing here?"

His grin broadens. "You in or out?"

I raise an eyebrow at him. "Well considering how many times we escaped death, I have to admit I'm feeling a little reckless..." Whispering so he has to strain to hear, I say, "*In.*"

He stops midstride, setting me back on my feet.

I use his body as an anchor, and lean onto his side.

"You'll have to step back for this one," he tells me.

Intrigued, I do as he wants. He begins fumbling with his hair and the skin around it. He's jabbing his skin, scratching and pulling. When something begins to break around his head, he makes an exaggerated sound of pain.

Pretending to glare at him, I say, "I'm *not* falling for that trick again." All I hear is a low chuckle before a piece of flesh comes off. Even though I know it's not real, I can't stop the gasp escaping my mouth.

"See?" He points to his forehead. "No blood." I'm confused for a second more before I finally realize what he's doing.

"It's a *wig,*" I exclaim, laughing.

He's shaking his head, letting the wind blow through his dark blonde hair. "All I know is that they're right. Red heads *do* have all the fun."

"So do you put that thing on every time you rescue a damsel in distress?" I guess, smiling.

"Yes." He gives me a wolfish grin, filled with mirth. I roll my eyes as Kaiden picks me up, settling me on his chest. We continue walking, and I notice that nothing is crumbling around us, and the wind isn't shrieking like a banshee. We're moving through dense bushes and trees, but I'm still worried it's not real.

"Have we passed Saguinox territory?"

"Yes. We're safe now," he says confidently.

"How can you be sure?" I ask, uncertain.

"This is the path I took to get in. It's owned by the gov-ernment, and hasn't been touched by the Saguinox."

"Do you think more will come for us tonight?" I ask, unable to stop the slight tremors rocking my body.

He holds me tighter. "I don't think so. They've been very secretive and busy. We were able to intercept a few of their messages," he informs me. Inhaling sharply, I wait anxiously for him to finish. "It was very clear the warriors would be gone this week. I'm not sure what's happening, but it's big." He looks down at me. "We knew I only had a short window to get them in and out."

"Them," I repeat slowly. "Do you mean Chloris... and Nymphora?"

"Yes."

"What do you guys do?"

"We're mercenaries."

What? I gasp.

"People hire us to do things for them."

I'm suspicious. "What sorts of things?"

He stops for a long moment. "Anything."

It's an ambiguous answer, and my mind is jumping to all sorts of terrible conclusions. I try to picture Chloris doing something like killing for money, but the image doesn't make sense. She seems too timid and nervous to do something like that. Maybe he's sensing what I'm thinking because he continues, "Some of us only do what we believe in. I've never done anything I've been afraid to admit to. This is something my family has always been a part of," he confides.

Nodding, I say, "Okay."

We continue in compatible silence for many minutes. Knowing that this isn't part of the Saguinox land, I breathe in fresh air, wondering how I've never notice how clean it is; how sweet it smells.

"Do you know what I want to do?" I ask.

"What?"

"I want to drive."

He laughs. "All right." His voice is amused. "Once your leg's good, you can drive again."

"I want to be in the city," I continue, my mind imagining the bright city lights. *I want to be around humans.*

"Mmmm." He makes the sound in my hair. We walk in silence for a long while. Even in the dark, I see charred skin on my palm. It hurts, and I open my hands, letting the wind wash over the pain.

Eventually, it gets so dark that Kaiden almost bumps into a tree. He laughs, but I'm the one who almost got hit. Taking a deep breath, I whisper, "Light." A tiny flame flickers above my open palm, swaying slightly underneath my breath. It's small, but it's better than nothing. I hold it up to help light the way.

"You'll burn me with that," Kaiden reminds me, moving his face to the side.

"Don't be such a baby. It's just a little fire."

He grunts, but he doesn't put his face near me again.

"Kenna, I want to tell you something," Kaiden abruptly begins after a lengthy silence. His voice is more serious than I've ever heard it. "It's very important so listen carefully." He takes a deep breath. My heart begins to hammer.

"This realm has always been filled with magic. There are hundreds of planets that magical creatures inhabit. Earth was the last to be formed, and the only planet left that has remained, for the most part, untainted by black magic. Earth has never been important because there was always greater power somewhere else." He stops. "Are you understanding?"

I'm dazed with all the information he's giving me. "Even after everything that's happened, it's so hard to believe it's real," I whisper, unable to fully convey the bewilderment, fascination, and pain of what I'm feeling.

"Aliens are *very* real," he states. "Every alien I've ever met has had magic. Don't let yourself be confused. It could cost you your life. Humans have a silly idea of what aliens are and what they look like. It's nothing close to the truth."

"You said there was always greater power somewhere else and that's why Earth has been left alone for so long," I recall. "The Saguinox have revealed themselves here. Does that mean--"

"Yes." His answer is sad and angry at the same time. "It means that power is here now." He takes another deep breath. "It means that they're here to stay."

"Why?" My question is a petrified whisper.

"That question has many answers. I don't know them all. This is what I do know. They've destroyed everything. Earth is the only planet left. To understand what that means we need to go back." He holds me tighter, as if I'm going to flee after I hear what he's about to say. "Thousands of years ago there used to be universal laws created by the Council. The Council was made up of powerful magicians from every race and every planet. They had in their possession something called the element crystals. No one knows how they came to posses these, but for as long as time has existed the Council has protected them. These crystals are energy sources that specifically control elements present in *all* the planets. To possess these would be to have powers over the *entire* universe. The crystals needed guardians, and were protected by the elemental witches. These were magical people who had an affinity for certain magic special to the crystal, like air, water, land which they called tierra, and... fire."

I stiffen in his embrace. Before I can say anything, he rushes on, continuing. "The Council wasn't perfect. Their intentions were always good, but corruption and power often rose to the surface of everything they did. Eventually it all fell apart, and when the Council disintegrated, the magic did, too. The crystals disappeared. No one could find them

"Then, a hundred and fifty years ago, rumors surfaced about some remarkable crystals. There were whispers that in order to protect them some elemental witches hid them *in people*. No one believed it for a long time. I mean how could you? It was crazy." Kaiden's voice shifts, growing darker and angrier. "Then the Saguinox began invading planets, and triumphing over every type of magic. That's when people started investigating. It's a long story, but the only thing you need to know is the Saguinox have the crystals."

He takes another deep breath, like he's trying to forget something painful. "We believe for a long time now they have been using the crystals to destroy their enemies. What they didn't know is that the crystals are wild magic. There's always a price to using them. They destroyed many planets before they finally understood, but by then it was too late. There was only one planet left, still untouched, still pure." His embrace tightens. "They have every crystal, except one. Someone hid it very well, and it's been lost ever since."

There was light and colors...

Like fire.

Remember.

"Me," I whisper.

He presses his face to me. "Yes," he reinforces quietly. "Kenna, you are the carrier of the fire crystal. You're the miracle we've all been hoping for."

CHAPTER 29

The stars suddenly look brighter than they've ever looked. I try to imagine somebody living there, someone using magic even. But it all sounds so unbelievable that the only image I can get in my head is E.T. riding his bike.

Kaiden is next to me, trying to sleep. He tells me he only needs an hour to regain his strength, but he's been knocked out for almost two so I'm not sure if he's telling the truth.

Its still night, and I wonder if it will ever be day again. The pain shooting up and down my body has intensified, but the throbbing in my head is worse. After the fire has cooled, my head is a field of dead brain cells. When Kaiden catches me massaging my head, he tells me the pain is normal. It hurts so bad what I really want to do is cut my head open with a rock. Would *that* be normal? Somehow I think not.

Soon, fatigue, pain- or maybe both- makes me drowsy. My eyelids are heavy like bricks, but I don't want to sleep. I'm scared about what I might see.

I play a game with myself to keep me awake. I make pictures with the stars, connecting them like dots. There's one star in particular shining brighter than the rest. For some reason, I'm drawn to it. My eyes keep returning to the star, staring at the sparkling white perfection, transfixed by its beauty.

The throbbing pain in my body is making me dizzy, but I don't stop. Gazing intently, I start to see something shift, moving gently. Lightheaded, I concentrate deeper until the faraway light seems to drift closer.

I should be afraid, but I'm not. I'm motionless, waiting for it.

Losing myself in the haze, I finally close my eyes.

CHAPTER 30

I'm in a tunnel.

The whiteness isn't a star.

Before I become alarmed, a deep voice says, "We really should stop meeting this way." Instantly, all fears evaporate. He's waiting for me at the end, a tall shadow in the startling brightness. Suddenly I feel lighter inside.

"Maybe you should visit more." I can't keep my tone as stern as I would like. Looking at his face makes my heart jump faster. "You know, instead of leaving me in a prison."

My sneakers produce soft sounds on the cement floor, and it reverberates gently like the noises of a grandfather clock. "FYI," I continue to inform him. "It ranks first on the list of worst ways to court a girl."

Rhys smiles, but doesn't reply. Inwardly, I sigh in dismay. He's so handsome, and has done the worst thing possible, yet my heart is still fluttering, aching to be held by him. Without a doubt I belong in the psych ward. *Maybe he hears me because he laughs, gazing at me with a strange tenderness.*

Ignoring how his expression makes my skin scorch, I ask, "Is this another dream? Or am I really dead this time?" My footsteps are loud in the serene silence as I come to stand by him.

"No," he answers softly. "You're not dead. Not yet, anyway."

"Comforting," I say as I reach him. There is light all around us in the tunnel, and it seems to go for miles and miles. "Where are we?"

He shrugs. "I'm not sure. The In- between maybe?"

"Another cryptic answer." I want to touch him, and so I do. Only this way can I say what I want, and feel him the way I want to. In real life it'd never be like this. It could never be like this.

His cheeks are firmer than I imagined, and I trace the bones lightly. He catches my hand, and presses his face into it. He flips it over, studying my palm. It's completely black. It's so dark my birthmark isn't visible. He looks angry. His scrutiny makes me uncomfortable, and I try to snatch my hand away.

"Killed a couple evil creatures today," I tell him lightly. "I think I should be promoted from sidekick to hero."

"I always knew you could do it."

"It would've been nice if you told me earlier, then I could've gotten out of that hell hole faster." This time my voice is stern.

"Your powers come when you're ready for them," he tells me. "They wouldn't have come any earlier than now."

"How do you know so much about me?"

"I make it my business to know things about beautiful women." He kisses the middle of my blackened palm tenderly. "Like this, for instance," he says, rubbing the spot where my birthmark is. "Where I come from, a mark defines who you are," he reveals quietly. "If you're a guard you're marked with that symbol. If you're a warrior, you're celebrated with that symbol." His eyes catch mine. "And if you are a carrier, then it's imprinted into your skin, hidden in your body." More questions swirl in my mind, but whenever I'm with Rhys like this they become less important.

Without looking away from me, he kisses each part of my birthmark until he reaches the end. His lips suck the tip of my index finger gently. I'm barely able to breathe, and hot chills wash over me with every kiss that he gives.

"Sometimes when you're afraid, all you have to do," he traces my scar again "is find your mark." His touch makes me ache.

"Rhys," I whisper. "How can we be together like this?"

"Magic."

I'm frustrated with his answer. "How come you always leave me when I need you the most?" My voice breaks.

"Sometimes the choices we make are not always the right ones, but they are the necessary ones for right now."

"Necessary? Imprisoning me is necessary? Letting someone hurt me is necessary?" I ask, shattered.

"I have to." His confession sounds pained. He grips my shoulders hard. "I feel everything you feel when you hurt, Kenna. I feel it. In here," he points to his head. "And in here." He points to his heart.

"Then leave and come with me!"

"I can't." For the first time he sounds angry with me. "There are things that are bigger than us. Everyone has a part, and I have to play mine."

"What is my part then?" I snap back. "Tell me. I'll do it. Anything for this nightmare to be over."

His lips clench together. "You're already doing your part."

I stare at him, livid, and sad at the same time. He's looking at me, too, and it's like we're each trying to stare the other down. Neither one of us wants to give in, but the fatigue in his eyes hurts my heart so I look away.

"Are you always going to stay with me in my head?" I ask quietly, staring ahead into the white nothingness.

"Only until you're part is done."

I want to screech at him, to tell him to stop playing these dangerous games. I want to shout at him be with me. Choose me. But I don't get a chance to say those things.

The second I turn to him, his lips crush mine. It's a forceful kiss, a kiss filled with frustration, anger, and injustice. He hurts me when his teeth nip my lips, but I want more. I crave the pain because it means he's real. It means he's just as shattered as I am.

I bury my fingers in his hair, reveling in how close I can pull him. When my whole body is pushed against his, I wrap my legs around his waist, forcing him to carry me the way my heart had been carrying him since the moment he saw me.

We pull away because the light is dimming around us. I know what he's going to say before he says it.

"Yes," I answer. "I'll survive. I'm a survivor," I echo his words.

He clutches me hard. "You need to believe it. Now is not the time for you to die."

Shadows cover us, slowly rising like mists. They get to him first, but before they can pull him away, he grabs my hands, touching my birthmark.

"This is who you are." His eyes stay on me until the last possible second.

When the blackness starts to pull me back, I'm afraid it's the last time I'll ever see him again.

CHAPTER 31

Jerking awake, I sputter, coughing hard. Something wet is rolling down from my mouth.

"What *is* that? What did you do?" I accuse, pushing Kaiden's hand away.

"Medicine."

"Are you sure? Because it tastes more like roots and bark," I say, wiping my mouth with my hands.

"That's because it is." Abruptly, I want to vomit. "Keep it in. You're getting a fever and you need it in your body."

"Ugh." I try to stand but I'm wobbly. His strong arms pull me up.

"We need to get you to a doctor. We're heading into the city now," he says.

Cheering considerably at his words, I brighten. "Where are we?"

"This facility's in Wisconsin. We're almost to Milwaukee." My face breaks into a huge grin. *I'm almost home!*

"Nymphora and Chloris are supposed to meet us there." If possible, my smile grows even wider. We made it. We're actually going to make it out alive. Then I think about whether anyone else has survived and I feel my smile slip, disappearing beneath my worry.

Kaiden notices and he squeezes my hand. The sky is getting lighter. I tell him we need to go. "I want to see the sun rise over the city," I breathe. I'm so excited I don't allow Kaiden to carry me, choosing to have him half drag me instead. I suddenly feel stronger. Kaiden points out smugly it's probably the medicine, but I know it's because my heart senses it's almost home.

We move in companionable silence, listening to the leaves rustle and the insects calling. Eventually the pain gets to me and Kaiden sweeps me in his arms. It's become such a familiar habit for me I know right where to put my head, and how to grasp his neck.

"When we get back I'm getting two Chipotle burritos," Kaiden says, breaking the amiable silence.

"I'm getting a Big Mac."

"I'm drinking a liter of coke," he continues.

"I'm eating ramen noodles."

He stops. "Really? That's not cool."

I shrug. "It reminds me of home."

We're slowly going up a slope. "Do you still want to see a sunrise?" he asks me. I smile radiantly at him. He bounces me in his arms, happy at my excitement.

"It'll be nice to see something man made," I say, thinking about our skyscrapers.

"Something that doesn't crumble."

Brightness flickers up ahead, and it can only be the sun making its way up. I vow to never take it for granted again. My heart is pounding with exhilaration. When we're close, I tell Kaiden to put me down. He obeys, laughing at my childish joy. We're on a hill overlooking the city.

I limp forward, desperate to see the city lights, dimming beneath a rising sun. When I finally get to the top, I halt. What I see brings me to my knees.

The city is in ruins.

Burning.

End of Book One

DEDICATION

To my parents who support me in everything I do. You both have taught me what it's like to love unconditionally and strive for my dreams. I'm forever grateful to be your daughter!

To Amanda and Samantha- a girl can't ask for better sisters. Amanda, thanks for always making time in your busy day to listen to me talk for "five minutes" and not complain when it turns into twenty. Samantha, thanks for reading all my drafts and supporting this double life I've started. You're the best! I love you both to infinity and beyond!

To Molly and Amy- the best cheerleaders! Molly, thanks for reading my story and making time to give me feedback. This book is what it is because of YOU! Amy, thanks for always being there and having my back when I need you the most. You two rock!

To TX: Thank you for giving me the push I needed to start writing.

To my personal life- I've missed you. We'll see each other soon. Maybe.

To Regina Wamba for creating a gorgeous cover. Is there anything you CAN'T do?

To all the amazing bloggers and fans out there who support indie authors. You're appreciated, adored, and thanked a thousand times over. You're awesome beyond words. Thank you!

Last, but not least, to YOU for picking up this book. You make the lack of sleep, stress, and hard work all worth it. Thank you for starting this journey with me. I promise there will be many more to come.

About the author

My name is Mari Arden (Mari- rhymes with safari). Teacher by day, author by night. I love my double life. You can also catch me at the gym attempting to sweat out all the sweets I eat when I write. Key word: TRY. I love sushi and Chipotle burritos, and wouldn't it be paradise if they could be combined somehow? Well on second thought, maybe not.

Adventurous? Come join my double life!

mariarden.blogspot.com

facebook.com/pages/
Mari-Arden-author/493749174011347

goodreads.com/author/show/6897452.Mari_Arden

twitter.com/mariarden

The Enchanted
Micalea Smeltzer

Coming Soon

CHAPTER ONE

Years.

I had waited years for this moment.

For this one perfect moment that was supposed to somehow complete me.

Now, that it was here, I found that it was lacking something. The royal blue graduation gown was rough against my skin and kept making this weird swooshing sound anytime I moved. I was itching like crazy in this heat. I wanted to fan myself but I was sure that Ms. Jones, the Assistant Principal, would cut off my arms if I attempted to. Matthew Pierson, who sat next to me, kept wiggling and trying to talk to Eddie Ralston on my other side. Ms. Jones shot daggers at Matthew while Mr. Taylor droned on and on about our futures.

Sweat trickled down my brow and into my eye, stinging it.

I'm on fire in more ways than one now; I thought glumly.

Wasn't graduation supposed to be this amazing day? Our lives tied up and shipped off to various colleges and universities? Parties? Fun?

Instead, I was spending the accumulation of the last thirteen years of my life drowning in my own sweat. When Mr. Taylor handed me my diploma I was going to find the nearest pool, lake, pond, river, sink, just the nearest water source would do, and drench myself with its coolness. I could just envision the cool water pouring over my skin. Maybe if I visualized hard enough I wouldn't need the pool.

"You have all worked hard to reach this day," Mr. Taylor continued. "Thirteen years-"

Matthew leaned across to me and snorted at Eddie. "It'll be another thirteen years before this speech is over."

"You've got that right," muttered Eddie.

Close but not quite. It was another thirteen minutes. By this point there was a puddle under my seat composed of my salty sweat. My makeup had long ago melted off.

Mr. Taylor smiled at us all, sweeping his arms in a grand gesture, and began to call out the names.

At least the graduating class was small.

Mr. Taylor soon made it to the P's and I breathed a sigh of relief. Not much longer now. I could hear the shower calling my name now.

"Matthew Arnold Pierson," he called. Matthew bound onto the stage, creating quite a show, much to the delight of the other football players.

"Mara Hadley Pryce," he said next. I breathed a sigh of relief. Me.

I walked up to the stage, much more graciously than Matthew had, although I had to keep telling myself not to run. Mr. Taylor shook my hand, handed me my diploma, and said, "Congratulations Mara."

Thirteen years for *this*, I thought. It was so... so... so anticlimactic. I mean, come on, give us some fireworks, some strobe lights, *something!*

But no.

All I got was sweat, cheap polyester, and "congratulations Mara."

I heard the sound of my dad hollering and whistling in the crowd. I would have been embarrassed if other parents hadn't made a bigger deal out of it.

I shook my head and shuffled off the stage where Ms. Jones moved my tassel over.

As I was walking back to my seat I noticed a guy leaning against the bleachers. I had never seen him before and this was a small town where everyone knew *everyone.*

He was tall and lean with dark wavy black hair and tan skin. Despite the summer heat he wore a black t-shirt and black jeans. It looked like he had a few tattoos. He wasn't smiling. In fact, he didn't seem happy at all. And his bright, gray eyes were staring right at me. Through me. It was like he was eating me alive. His eyes narrowed.

I blinked and he was gone which left me believing he had been a figment of my imagination. And I might have believed that, if I hadn't chosen that moment to glance at my dad. He was standing. Stopped mid-clap, and looking at the empty space by the bleachers, with a horror stricken look on his face.

I shook my head and all but fell into my chair. I tried to forget about the dark haired boy.

Mr. Taylor went down the list and finally called the last person.

Before I knew it our caps were flying in the air.

Thirteen years of schooling over in a matter of minutes.

The class cheered and we all stood in a collective burst of royal blue and bright sunlight yellow.

"Mara!" cried Dani crashing into me.

"Whoa!" I said, steadying us before I fell into someone, and started a human game of dominos.

"It's over!" she sobbed, and I realized she was crying. "We're all going our separate ways! What if we never see each other again! Mara, please tell me that won't happen!" she pulled on my gown and I worried she would rip it. It was a rental and there was no way I could afford to pay for repairs.

"Dani," I said, in a soothing voice like a parent would use with a child. "That's not going to happen. We've known each other since kindergarten. I'm not going to throw all those years away. Besides, I've tried to get rid of you before. You're not easily thwarted," I joked.

She smacked me on the arm and wiped her face free of tears. Her white blond hair was long and straight and hung down her back like a curtain. She was small and pixie like. Her face was narrow and pointed but she was beautiful. I never understood why she wanted to be friends with plain old me.

I had light, fly away, brown hair. Freckles dotted my nose and my upper lip was bigger than my lower lip with a partial gap between my two front teeth. Dani thought the gap was very vogue. I thought it was annoying. I was average height, five foot six, and hippy. Not tall and slender like Dani. Even though I was almost eighteen, I still had a child-like quality to me and I hated it.

Dani could have hung out with the popular crowd but instead she stuck by me. I had yet to figure out what was so great about me.

"Are you going to go to Jules party?" she asked.

"I don't want to," I whined.

"Pretty please?" she pouted. She had been pestering me all week to go to Jules' graduation party tonight. I wasn't the party type but Dani enjoyed them and always wanted me to go with her.

"If I give in will you leave me alone?" I asked.

"Thank you, thank you, *thank you!*" she squealed and hugged me.

"You owe me," I laughed, her good mood rubbing off on me.

"I know! But I'm too happy to care!" she cried clapping her hands.

The parents were now making their way down to us from the bleachers. Many of them were fanning themselves with programs. I could feel my hair fuzzing around my head from the humidity.

I saw my dad heading towards me, and Dani's parents were behind him.

"Congrats kiddo," dad wrapped his arms around me. His brown hair was receding from his forehead leaving a bald patch and his brown eyes sparkled with happiness.

I had his light brown hair; it was the only piece of resemblance we shared but I still wished I had my mom's beautiful auburn locks.

"Thanks dad," I said.

"I sure wish your momma coulda' been here to see this."

"Me too," I said, even though it didn't make a difference to me. My mom had died when I was a baby. All I had to remember her by was one lone picture and a mysterious box I wasn't allowed to open until my twentieth birthday. It was all very twilight zone to me.

"She'd be so proud of you, baby girl," he kissed my forehead. "I know I am. I'm proud of you too, Dani," my dad called to my best friend where she stood a little ways over with her parents.

"Thanks Mr. Pryce."

"How many times have I told you, Dani? Call me Steven," he said. "Mr. Pryce makes me feel old."

"Dad, you could never be old," I said.

He chuckled. "That's what you think. You're young," he said. "Where do you want to go for dinner?" he asked me.

Before I could answer him Dani came over. "Uh- Mr. Pryce, I mean Steven, Mara and I are going to a party," she said sweetly. "We could really use this time to get ready."

My dad sighed. "I get it. You don't want to be seen with your old man. It's okay, Mara," he said.

I glared at Dani and turned back to my dad. "I have plenty of time to eat and get ready. I don't take five hours like *some* people," I pointed over my shoulder at Dani.

My dad instantly perked up.

"Good, good," he said. "Shall we go?"

"Yeah," I said. "Dani, do you want to get ready at my house or do you want me to come over?"

She eyed me. "My house. You have no fashionable clothes. I'll need to dress you."

"Great," I said, with false enthusiasm.

She laughed and danced away calling, "Ta, ta," over her shoulder.

"Come on kiddo," dad said, and slung his arm around me. "Let's get rid of this thing," he tugged on my blue gown, "and get something to eat. I'm starving," he patted his stomach.

I laughed. "Sounds like a plan. Why don't you go wait in the truck and I'll meet you there?"

"Alright, kid," dad said and left me.

I followed the mass of student into the school to the gymnasium where we would return our gowns. I found myself unconsciously looking for the mysterious dark haired boy. I'd have to remember and ask my dad about him during dinner.

Once in the gym, I had to wait in line to return the cumbersome gown.

"Hey, Mara?" said a voice behind me.

I turned around. Eli stood behind me. Eli was a football player, tall, broad shoulders, brown hair, green eyes, and the school hunk. But he liked me for whatever reason. Maybe it was because I was 'hard to get' when really I just wasn't interested. I mean, Eli was a nice guy, especially for a popular football player, but he wasn't my type. In fact, I wasn't sure I even had a type.

"Hi Eli," I said.

"Man, was it hot outside or what?" he said.

"Yep," I said, nodding my head. I tried to send out not so subtle *go away*, vibes.

"Uh-" he glanced around nervously. "Are you going to Jules' party?" he asked and rubbed the back of his head.

Apparently, my vibes weren't working.

"Yeah," I said.

He smiled. "Me too. Maybe I'll see you there?"

I was saved from answering by one of the teachers calling me over to take my gown. I handed the blue fabric to her, she checked my name off the list, and I dashed out to the parking lot before Eli could find me and continue our conversation.

Dani thought I should just go for him. But I didn't see the point in wasting my time or his.

Dad's old Ford Ranger idled outside the front of the school. The old red paint was more of a brown color now thanks to rust and chipped paint.

He had the windows rolled down and a country song playing on the radio. I opened the door and climbed inside. "Where to kid?" he asked putting the truck into gear.

"How about Mammies?" I asked, naming off a local diner.

He grinned. "You read my mind."

He finagled his way into the line of exiting vehicles and honked his horn and stuck his head out the window to yell at various drivers that he deemed either too slow, too fast, too arrogant, or too something.

My dad's driving antics always made me laugh. It was always and adventure when he was driving.

"I declare," my dad said, now safely cruising down a main thoroughfare, "people do not know how to drive these days."

I laughed. "Dad, maybe it's *you* who doesn't know how to drive."

"Nonsense," he waved his hand. His gold wedding band reflected in the sunlight.

My mom had been dead for almost eighteen years and in that time my dad had never dated anyone. Whenever I asked him why, he would look at me thoughtfully, and say, "Your momma was the love of my life. I'll never find another love like hers."

Sometimes I wished he would date; get any kind of so-cial life, so he wouldn't be so involved in mine. But other times I was thankful that my dad was so present in my life. We were close and had an unbreakable bond.

As the truck cruised down the road my hair swirled around my face. I had to keep batting it away and pulling it out of my mouth. My dad thought it was funny.

He pulled into Mammies and parked the truck. He took up two parking spots, but in dad's book that was okay. I hopped out and followed him inside. He picked our usual booth and didn't even bother opening a menu.

Jessica, the lone waitress, came over and leaned against the booth.

"The usual?" she asked.

My dad grinned. "Of course."

Jessica grabbed the menus off the table and disappeared into the kitchen. A moment later she returned with a Dr. Pepper for me and a Bud Light for my dad.

I slurped the brown liquid down. I was so thirsty from sitting out in the Arkansas heat for the last while. I pulled my hair back into a ponytail and secured it with a band off my wrist. Little wisps of hair still managed to escape and hang in my face. Oh well.

Jessica came back to the table with a refill of Dr. Pepper and a basket of fresh rolls. I grabbed one up and slathered it with butter, before devouring it. I hadn't realized I was hungry until we got here.

"Slow down, Mara. You're going to choke yourself," dad chuckled.

"Hungry," I mumbled around a mouthful of roll.

Dad laughed. "That's very ladylike Mara," he said.

"Bite me," I growled.

"Girls," he muttered. "Why couldn't I have had a son?"

"Because I'm awesome and way better than any boy," I swallowed. I added a flip of my hair for emphasis.

My dad laughed. "Mara, Mara, Mara," he sighed.

"Oh," I said, swallowing a bite of bread. I took a swig of soda for good measure. "Did you know that guy, the one with the dark hair and clothes, leaning against the bleachers?"

"I didn't see anyone," he said, way too quickly.

I narrowed my hazel eyes at him. "Really? I saw you looking at him."

"No," he said, "I saw no one."

I swallowed some more soda and stared at my dad. I knew I saw the boy, and he had definitely been looking at him too. So why was he acting like the guy didn't exist? It was peculiar to say the least.

Jessica came out with our food. A B.L.T. and fries for me and an artery clogging cheese burger for my dad.

My dad bit into his burger, chewed, and said, "I don't know what I'll do with you off at college next year. I'll sure miss you baby girl."

"Dad," I whined. "Don't make me cry. I have all summer with you. Don't say goodbye yet. Besides," I added, "I'm still going to be living at home and working around here. I'm only taking one class." One class was, sadly, all I could afford.

My dad patted my hand. "It's never too soon to say goodbye. Remember that, Mara."

"What do you mean?" I asked.

He swallowed. "I just mean that. Sometimes you don't have a chance to say goodbye."

"You're talking about mom aren't you?"

He sighed. "Of course... among other things."

His eyes kept darting around the restaurant. It was strange behavior for my father. He wasn't normally so jumpy. I found myself constantly looking over my shoulder, expecting some kind of trouble.

Jessica came by with the ticket and dad couldn't get it paid and out of there fast enough.

On the way home he kept glancing in the rearview mirror. But I never saw anything.

Made in the USA
Lexington, KY
24 March 2013